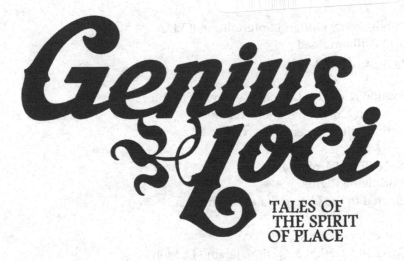

## TALES OF
## THE SPIRIT
## OF PLACE

# Edited by
# Jaym Gates

Published by Outland Entertainment LLC
3119 Gillham Road
Kansas City, MO 64109

Founder/Creative Director: Jeremy D. Mohler
Editor-in-Chief: Alana Joli Abbott
Senior Editor: Gwendolyn Nix

ISBN: 978-1-947659-44-5
Worldwide Rights
Created in the United States of America

Editor: Jaym Gates
Cover Illustration & Design: Jeremy D. Mohler
Interior Layout: Mikael Brodu

Printed and bound in the United States of America.

Visit **outlandentertainment.com** to see more, or follow us on our Facebook Page facebook.com/outlandentertainment/

# CONTENTS

# — EDITOR'S NOTE —
## Jaym Gates

**W**hen Brooke Bolander and I started discussing the weird *genius loci* of the places we grew up in a Facebook thread, we had no idea it would turn into an anthology (yes, I feel like this is a recurring theme). The concept of *genius loci* is something close to both of us. Brooke talks about her background in the introduction.

My background was as weird and rural, set in Northern California to her Texas. Clark Ashton Smith, Jack London, and Mark Twain all took inspiration from the area I grew up in. The hills there are known colloquially as *Calabama*, a strange mix of the Deep South, the Wild West, and remote mountains.

My hometown still relies on logging, mining, and ranching to keep it afloat. If our horses got off our property, they could get lost for weeks in the government-owned wildlands behind us. Family trips were spent in Death Valley, the Desolation Wilderness, and other remote locations. The ranchers rode with guns on their saddles, and when fires swept the mountains near my town last year, ranchers loaded horses and dogs into their trailers and headed into mountain meadows to try to rescue the stock.

When I was ten or so, the bridge on our road washed out, leaving us with only a single way out: a treacherous, muddy road winding back through the hills. When I was eighteen months old, an unseasonable snowstorm nearly trapped my family in the mountains during a backpacking trip.

I respect the land, and have learned to listen when it speaks. It turns out that I'm not the only one. A lot of people jumped on the conversation, telling their own stories and asking for recommendations for reading. I was sure there had to be a dozen anthologies with this theme already, but, to my surprise, we seemed to be the first.

Authors started signing up, and a beast was born. Ragnarok Publications agreed to take a chance on it, and a brilliant team of slushers, advisors, and supporters shaped up around it.

It was a challenge to wrangle from the start. We received almost a million words in submissions, and the quality was amazingly high. Pretty sure I could have published three or four anthologies and all of them would have been good. But I didn't have that much room, and I had to whittle it down to the 111,000 words you're about to read.

A collection like this is an once-in-a-lifetime opportunity for an editor. It's a dream project, something I was able to take a risk producing. The Kickstarter goals focused on giving the authors more, making the project better and bigger and lusher, rather than on giving the backers a lot of physical stuff. It could easily have failed, although it is now becoming a nicely common Kickstarter strategy.

It's a diverse, eclectic collection. Some of the stories won't read as a genius loci story the first time around. Some are challenging, some are scary, or bleak. Many are based on real events. Some were strangely prophetic.

Take, for example, Ken Liu's *Snow Train*. He sent this story to me in the summer of 2014. The real Snow Train hadn't been brought out for years. Winter 2014, Boston was buried in a record-breaking snowstorm, and the train was brought out to help break Boston's public transit system out of the snow packs. Maybe it wouldn't have broken down if Charlie had been operating it.

Not every story will resonate with you, and that's okay. But I firmly believe that each story will resonate with *someone*, that each has something to say about our world and its strange spirits.

I hope, if nothing else, that it makes you look at the world around you and wonder what, *who*, is watching you.

Jaym Gates
August, 2014

# — INTRODUCTION —
## Brooke Bolander

When I was a kid, the land was alive and it had a bad attitude. I don't mean that it was alive in some sort of woo-woo, Grandmother Willow kind of way. It didn't talk or sing, and the loblollies didn't shape themselves into special messages just for me. It made itself known in different ways. Horses, for example, it was not particularly fond of. The total number of horses struck by lightning on that parcel of acreage was a little ridiculous, and the ones not zapped by the sky went on to broken legs and god knows what other manners of gruesome fate. Or maybe it just didn't like anything with hooves. At least one cow fell down a sinkhole (A deep, round ravine in the woods, tree roots jutting out all the way down like those hands in *Labyrinth*) and had to be winched back out by my grandfather, who dutifully tried to nurse the broken thing back to health with limited success. When she finally went to wherever cattle go when they shuffle off this mortal coil, he hitched her corpse to a tractor and dragged it to the back forty boneyard, a skull-studded expanse of pasture that served as a sky burial place for all our dearly departed livestock.

Or maybe it just didn't like *anything*. My mother swore she heard someone (something) whispering our names outside her bedroom window late one night, which was a good six feet off the ground and at least five miles from the nearest neighbor. One of my earliest memories is of a low, rhythmic drumming noise coming from the woods around our place. My folks said it was probably an oil derrick, and for all I know they were entirely correct, but I've never heard anything like it since, and it seemed to fade the older I got. An inebriated joyrider wrecked his car a few miles up the blacktop at 3 AM one night and somehow managed to stagger all the way to our porch, where he briefly pounded on the door, then wandered on. The bloodstains stayed in the wood until we moved and the porch was torn down.

And then there was my much more recent encounter with The Thing That Laughed. It was 2 in the morning deep in the piney woods hinterland, a cold and rainy September. Something laughed below my open second-story window. I say *something* because it was guttural and unhinged and not a coyote or owl or loon or cougar or fox or any other animal native to the Southeastern United States. I promptly got up and closed the damned window.

Most of this stuff is weird, but not unexplainable. People wreck their cars all the time. Horses and cows break their legs without any help from malevolent forest spirits pretty regularly, and oil derricks make weird noises that a six-year old could totally misinterpret as distant drums. My internal Scully understands these things. My internal *Mulder* knows how the land there felt and feels, how many graves are in those woods, how many headstones and abandoned homesteads and tumbledown shacks and Caddo burial mounds you stumble across if you hack your way through the blackberry brambles and vines. Loblolly pines grow fast. They cluster around the little one-horse road ruts of Eastern Texas like coyotes waiting for a mule to die, itching to pull down the sad Walmarts and empty courthouse squares and dying local businesses. This is *True Detective* territory, Joe Lansdale country, the place Leadbelly sang about going where the sun never shines. Cue swelling cicadas and the sound of a glass slide moaning down makeshift guitar strings. The South is constantly rotting down 'round your ears, damp and sweaty. How could that sort of omnipresent decay NOT inspire a gothic tradition? There was no way in all the humid, Spanish moss-encrusted hells I could grow up there and not escape carrying at least a little bit of superstitious dread.

All places have their own special personalities. The primeval forests of the Pacific Northwest don't feel the same as the ancient redwood groves of Northern California. Boston isn't New York isn't DC. Take a train from England into Scotland and you sense the landscape's mood changing almost as soon as you cross from Northumberland into Berwickshire. Some of this is geographical and environmental, obviously, but that doesn't always take into account the effect those shifting tones, that watchful feeling. Whether it's our innate desire as primates to put a face on everything or something other that can't be quantified, the way it moves us is very real, and calling it the 'spirit' of the place is as good a way to classify that unclassifiable feeling as any. The Romans knew it. The *genius loci* was the protector of an area, the spirit of the land that kept an eye on the land. You laid out offerings for your local forest god, or built a shrine dedicated to them, or splashed some wine or blood, because respecting the place you live is always a damned fine idea (you don't want to be on the bad side of a swamp or a city). More recently, there's a fine tradition of fanciful media devoted to the idea, from *the Haunting of Hill House* to *Mononoke Hime* to the book you're holding in your hands.

This anthology is our contribution to that tradition and our libation, collected and spilled in honour of all the places we've interacted with and been affected by. Long may they haunt our memories and hearts and the hairs on the back of our necks, rusted and gnarled and old as stone and the sky.

Brooke Bolander

# — THE CITY —
## Vivienne Pustell

The term "intelligent city" is a relatively new term, and one that isn't fully defined. Essentially, an intelligent city uses digital technology to improve life in the city. A digital city uses digital services to provide services. An intelligent city does this as well, but also can adapt to changing services. An intelligent city combines human, collective, and artificial intelligence with an emphasis on innovation and adaptation. While the term involves human input, it's easy to extrapolate from the concept of an intelligent city and picture a city which is sentient, buildings and networks providing a kind of body and brain beyond that of its human residents.

Examples of intelligent city concepts can be found in Amsterdam and Singapore, where designers integrate a variety of systems to measure energy use in real time with a goal of reducing CO2 emissions. In Singapore, this information is used to determine road fees, with the fees rising and falling based on use. In Amsterdam, it allows for efficient streetlights and tram stops. The key component in both cases is the fact that many systems are working together, in conjunction with human behavior and input. For instance, for the Singapore system to work, it has to involve urban logistics, cars that are equipped with technology that can integrate them into the grid, and mass transit systems that work with the grid. Sometimes high tech ideas are combined with low tech solutions—for instance, Chicago uses a low-tech solution of providing older homes with new windows and new lighting to reduce energy use. When combined with smart energy meters this saves millions of dollars in energy costs.

The idea of a city in which all systems communicate on a smart grid is both alluring and frightening. In the chilling story, "The City", Vivienne Pustell pictures a city that is not just intelligent—it's alive, and deeply menacing. The cause of the city's sentience is not stated, but one can imagine a city which becomes so "smart" that it becomes the ultimate Artificial Intelligence.

◄●►

T he scratching was distant; she breathed a little more easily for the time being.

She was crouched by a pile of rubble, digging through the concrete chunks with determination. There was usually a package here. This cache seemed to go unnoticed more than others. Farther from the walls, maybe.

Behind her, the jagged tips of the ruined skyscrapers gnawed ineffectually at the starless gray dome that used to be a sky. A few windows flickered with the meager light of candles or lanterns, but the never-ending twilight glow of the sky was usually enough illumination to get by. Besides, it was better not to draw attention.

She shifted a larger chunk of concrete gingerly, trying not to make a sound. A few pebbles rolled down the side of the pile and skittered across the street, echoing in the silence; she cringed.

The City made no noise. It loomed above and around the tiny figures creeping through the streets, but it would not speak to them. The silence pounded down on them. Some cried, but their cries were soon consumed; the noises vanished. The City did not like voices.

There was only the scratching to pierce the silence, but it was worse. The scratching, a distant sound of claws in rubble or pulling down more buildings, crafting more ruin, was always a sound of despair. With it came the breathing, the rough sound of an animal tracking a scent. A hungry animal.

If she could just find the cache.

The scratching was moving. The breathing was there.

Her heart thudded in her chest, but even that was somehow without noise. The City did not like heartbeats.

There! The edge of the cache became visible underneath a small slab of drywall. The worn canvas, tattered and weathered, almost blended into the pile of debris. Her breath caught in her throat, she gently eased up the drywall and lifted out the parcel.

The scratching was getting closer. The breathing was picking up pace; it had caught a scent and was honing in on it.

She cradled the parcel against herself, leaping out of the pile of rubble and into the middle of the street. She whipped her head to each side, searching. The street was empty. The oppressive weight of the silence syruped into her lungs and filled her throat. The buildings loomed over her, the judgmental eyes of the vacant windows staring down, challenging her. What right had she to be there?

The air was still. Her skin prickled, the hair on her exposed arms rising up from between a lattice of bright red scars.

Clutching the parcel against her chest, she ran. Her feet pounded the cracked road, even the thudding of her heavy boots muffled by the City.

The ringing was beginning in her ears. They were stinging, the high pitched whine, still so quiet, piercing into her skull. As the breathing and the scratching got closer, she knew, the ringing would get more persistent.

The skyscrapers shivered, arching over her and leaning in on her, fingers closing in tight to capture a victim. She was vermin, and the City's exterminator drew near, snuffling and slobbering with insatiable hunger.

She ran faster, leaping over piles of debris and forgotten possessions, her heart battering itself against her ribcage as she ran through the skeleton of the City.

A shadow—so brief it could have just been a blink—passed over her. She swallowed. There were no shadows in the City; there was no light but the glow of the sky, and that was too ubiquitous to cause shadows. Only in buildings was there darkness, but nowhere were there shadows.

A block ahead of her, she saw a figure. It was a faint silhouette, nebulous and swaying slightly, as if caught in an ocean current distantly remembered.

The figure was nearly gone. She could see a stop sign, skewed at a rough angle, through the figure's torso. It was wispy and ethereal, and one arm was completely gone. It swayed mindlessly.

She skidded to a stop, staring at the other person. She opened her mouth, then closed it, slowly backing up.

It heard the sound of her skidding and craned its head. A mournful face, already partially dissolved, stared toward her, only the eyes still fully corporeal. Pain and confusion flowed out at her. She thought she saw its mouth move, a desperate attempt to figure out how to form words.

"I'm sorry," she whispered, her voice catching in her throat. "I'm sorry." She spun on her heel and darted into the nearest building, collapsing to the floor as soon as she was fully into the darkness. She curled against the cold wall, bracing herself as the scratching came louder. The breathing was faster and harder. The ringing intensified; her skull felt like it might split.

She ripped off her shirt and balled it up, stuffing it into her mouth. She bit down hard to keep from screaming, her arms wrapped around her head in desperation.

Names were the first things lost.

No one understood, at first. People gathered together, trying to comfort each other, find loved ones, make meaning. It took so long to find the connection between the slow losses and the scratching, the breathing, the buildings closing in to bite. People became as jagged and ruined as the buildings.

First they lost their names, and everyone else's names too. They lost the name of the City.

They didn't know why they were there. They didn't know who they belonged to. They didn't remember, and they started to fade.

Entire families would watch each other vanish, the scratching and the ringing carving away their sanity even as the people they were standing next to lost limbs, became more and more translucent till eventually they became wispy and faded away. Their families watched and didn't know why they felt so profoundly sad. They didn't remember that there had been anyone there a few minutes ago. They faded away too, soon after.

No one made a sound, that's what she remembered. Even when people first clustered together, desperate to cling to each other and make sense of what had happened, the voices were muted and choked. The City took that, so that the names would be easy to steal. What good is a name if you can't use it?

She supposed that at some point she had a name. Perhaps there had even been people who brought her joy by saying it. She had been alone for a while. It didn't take long for people to realize that when they gathered, the vanishing came more quickly. The City saw their weakness, and delighted in it.

But it isn't so simple to destroy people. Take voices and take companionship and take memories, but people will fight back. They forged new ways of communicating—hidden caches throughout the rubble where they hid their weapons. Survival meant isolation. The caches were the only way to communicate, the only way to cling to the last vestiges of human connection.

She uncurled from against the wall, her heartbeat returned to normal and her breathing steady. With fingers that shook only slightly, she untied the tired, fraying cord from around the parcel. She pulled back the canvas and her lips curved up at the corners.

On the floor in front of her were weapons. Some jars of homemade paint. A carefully sharpened bit of glass. Some scraps of brilliantly colored fabric, stained but still vibrant.

She began with the fabric, ripping bits of her drab gray clothing and looping the cloth through so that it could be tied in place. Bits of pink clashed alongside safety orange, while a brilliant red bandana around her head warred with the yellow ribbons laced into her hair.

Next, the paint. She dipped her fingers into the jars, smearing her clothing and skin with the slimy gunk. It was no professional compound, for sure, but it dried and remained crusted, which was all that she needed.

Flames of color licked at her, but she knew it was not enough.

The final step was the glass. She gritted her teeth and quickly slashed across her arms several times, fresh red lines surging into existence, the older, gentler scars fading into the background at the aggression of the new gouges.

She squeezed her eyes closed for a moment. This was the choice she made. This was the choice they made, the people. They fought for themselves. They clung to some belief, vain or not, that it meant something.

She carefully screwed the top back onto the jar and wiped the glass on her clothes. They were put back into the canvas, along with the few remaining scraps of fabric, and everything was tied up again, a grungy gift of survival for the few.

She would return it to the pile where she had found it, so that someone else who knew about the drop could use it. Then, she would strike out to find more things to hide. She was better at finding food than finding color; she tried to leave provisions in the drops where she collected colors.

Sometimes she would see another person and their eyes would meet briefly. They would nod, but that would be all—they would have to hurry on their way before they aroused suspicion or drew attention. A brief meeting of eyes and a tiny nod could sustain her through cold nights and empty drops, when she ran low on color and couldn't close her eyes for fear of the scratching.

As she stood back up from burying the parcel back beneath the debris, she saw another figure. This one, unlike the last one, was distinct. It was another woman, tall and poised for flight, standing on the tattered remains of a fire escape across the street.

The woman blazed with color, from the paint and the fabric that graced her clothes to the rich caramel of her skin.

She looked up at the woman, their eyes meeting. They held the gaze for several seconds, never breaking the silence as they spoke. They nodded.

Then like that, the woman was gone, running down the street in a flare of color.

Watching down the street till the other woman was out of sight, she finally started walking in the opposite direction. She was tired; she hadn't slept well in days, and at long last she had enough color that she could sleep safely for a few hours. She had her armor against the vanishing; the ringing would wake her up before all her pigment was gone and the City could start to truly eat her.

No one had ever tried to defeat it.

Well, she supposed, perhaps someone had, but no one remembered. Perhaps those memories got eaten up.

But then, she suspected, everyone was too busy trying to stay corporeal to worry about truly fighting back. It was hard enough to not disappear; it was hard enough to keep what you had. Who could focus on fighting when there was surviving to be done? Fighting was the dream of course—when she sat, assuaging her loneliness with thoughts of eye contact and nods, she dreamed of fighting, of winning. But how could she fight the City?

She stood in the street, looking up. The sky was dispassionate, refusing her the comfort of warmth, refusing her the solace of darkness. It was always there, always looming. More than a sky, it seemed a lid—there is no exit that way. If it felt anything, it was sadistic humor, the spiked teeth of skyscrapers showing its twisted smile. The silence was the City laughing.

How could she fight? She couldn't touch her enemy; it had no face for her to punch.

She frowned. A few quick steps took her from the center of the street to the side of a building. She reached out one hand slowly, touching just the tips of her fingers to the cool wall. Lightly, then more firmly, she pressed her whole hand against it.

A faint smile flickered on her face for a moment.

Suddenly determined, she began striding down the street. She had a destination in mind; there was another cache nearby.

The City felt her confidence; the windows had seen her smile, brief though it was. The scratching began, and it was moving quickly. The breathing was full of lust, wet and slobbering with anticipation.

She walked more quickly, willing herself not to run. She would not run.

The buildings shivered and arched, the ringing splashing off of them maniacally.

"No," she whispered, but the syrup-thick air ate her words and filled her throat.

She ran.

The scratching followed, the sound of kitten claws on a floor, all excitement for the game.

She wove around piles of rubble in the street, her heart pounding silently in her chest. Her breathing was ragged, and she knew that she should have been making a sound, but there was no sound. Nothing but scratching, breathing, ringing.

The ringing clanged like a bell and was silent.

She held her breath. Everything was so silent.

The ringing picked back up again, the scratching now angrily clawing. The buildings were gnashing their teeth, but they were eager to chew on something else.

She slowed and skidded to a stop, warily turning around, afraid of what she might see.

At the last intersection was the woman she had seen before, fearlessly blazing with brilliant color, her head held high, her clothes swirling around her in a vibrant halo. She was walking away from the ringing with measured steps—still moving quickly, but moving without fear.

The ringing was angry, the breathing fast and hungry.

The woman remained defiant in her stride, her chin up.

The teeth were ready to gnaw, the buildings shivering and shaking.

The woman seemed unstoppable.

A wall collapsed forward, the cement tumbling down on the woman, pinning her legs to the ground. At first she struggled, but it took only a few moments for her resolve to crumble, her face dissolving and her posture going concave.

The breathing was laughter, the ringing a triumphant peal.

She began backing up very slowly, her eyes still fixed on the woman. The woman's mouth was open, but no sound came out. The woman's vanishing from the world would happen without mark, only the victorious trumpeting of the enemy for dirge.

The color of her clothing was fading, draining away. The color was a good defense—it took the City longer to eat them, they were less easily destroyed. But it was only a way of delaying, maybe buying the time to flee, to hide. It wasn't enough.

The woman's clothing would turn gray. The paint would disappear. Her skin would fade to gray and white, all the richness gone. And the woman would vanish.

She couldn't watch the woman fade. She felt the urge to stay, to try to offer some support or solidarity as the woman vanished, but she couldn't do it. She couldn't stay and watch, to see the woman's strength disappear... She couldn't risk herself for a pointless gesture.

The woman was lost; the City was feasting on her in a cacophony of ringing and breathing and gnashing teeth; it was safe to walk away and not look back, for she was too insignificant to take away from such a victory.

Never before had the absence of sound felt so cruel and kind at once. The echo of solitary footsteps should have been there to force her to face her isolation; the silence shielded her instead. Where there's no sound, one does not have to deal with the sounds of being singular.

She would continue with her plan. She had been going to the cache, and so she would keep going.

The cache wasn't far. She cut through some buildings to keep off the street, and soon arrived at what had once been a small park. There had been a playground for children, but now the tunnel slide was a popular drop for small canvas-wrapped parcels.

The parcel was there, bulging with supplies. It was fresh.

She curled into the mouth of the slide, barely squeezing into the gray plastic. Bruised fingers tugged the string that held the canvas wrapping on, releasing the fabric to fall away and reveal the contents: six jars of paint, all freshly filled.

The whisper of a smile passed across her face again for a moment, but, like everything in the City, it soon vanished and was forgotten.

She tied up the paints again and slid out of the slide. She couldn't think of the woman, not now. She couldn't indulge her loneliness. For now, there was only her, her paint—and the City.

She napped, and awoke feeling truly rested. She was reinvigorated.

Paint smears on her body and hands affirmed that what she had done had not been a dream. She jumped up, slinging the parcel of paints over her shoulder with a makeshift strap she had fashioned; always carrying the paints in her hands was inconvenient.

The scratching seemed far away; she was surprised. She trotted along, alert and wary.

She slowed and then stopped. Her face filled with a glow of satisfaction.

The paint smears across the buildings were huge. She had climbed and stretched and covered almost an entire story.

Across the front of one building, "HELLO."

Across the street, "I AM STILL HERE."

The letters were large and jagged, made out of multiple colors of paint—messy, haphazard, clashing. She didn't care. She felt a swell of pride in her chest; she thought it was beautiful.

It had worked. She didn't know if the paint would fade away on the buildings, but there it was, hours after she had painted it. Her idea worked.

Filled with new resolve, she moved a few blocks further to a small square. There was a smooth glass-fronted building on one side. She took the parcel of paints from her shoulder and spread them out before her. There was more to be done.

The scratching was nearly on top of her.

She was struggling to scrape enough paint out of the last jar to finish the last letter when she realized it. Her task had so absorbed her; her guard had dropped.

She looked at the wall, to her hands, to the jar of paint, to the sky—to the scratching. How had she not noticed that the buildings surrounding this square formed a sadistic smirk in the sky?

She stared at the teeth, could feel their eagerness to eat her.

The breathing slobbered, its hunger matching the teeth.

"No," she whispered. "No," she repeated, her voice getting stronger.

She clawed at the inside of the jar, scraping up every last bit of paint.

"You don't win!" Her voice was shaky, but she spoke; she did not whisper.

Her hands slathered the paint on the wall, smearing what little she had as far as she could. The last letter was uglier, weaker than the last. But it was there.

The scratching was there. The ringing shrilled in her ears, piercing into her.

She turned and stood, hands on her hips, back to her creation.

"I AM FIGHTING" blazed across the glass.

The scratching seemed to falter for a moment, as if it had tripped. The lusty breathing paused.

She stood, trying to swallow her fear.

The scratching began again, angrier.

There was rage in it. It knew.

Her breathing was fast and shallow.

Running was futile.

Her clothes were already fading.

There was no paint left in the jar. None of the jars.

The buildings were tightening.

She could feel herself shrinking.

"No no no," she whispered.

The breathing snuffled with delight; a laugh of triumph.

She was fraying, she knew it.

The ringing pealed in victory.

Her hand curled in her pocket.

"No," she whispered again, clutching at her voice.

She pulled her hand from her pocket, her fingers holding a shard of glass.

The scratching paused. The ringing fell silent.

"This ends—on my terms!" she snarled, her voice ghostly and ragged—but hers.

The scratching, the breathing, the ringing, the buildings—they all came together and the City raged and clawed and bit.

She held the glass above her wrist.

Her body was fading; her insides were disintegrating; her thoughts were fleeting.

She was still fighting.

She pressed the glass down.

# — THE GRUDGE —
## Thoraiya Dyer

*Once upon a time (in 1954, to be exact), two brothers in Beirut inherited two plots of land, one in front of the other. The plot in front was largely earmarked for road development, and therefore was virtually useless. The brothers planned to combine the two plots, but they could not agree on how to do it. Eventually their arguments became so heated that the brother with the smaller plot hired two architects (who, coincidentally, were also brothers) to design a tall but narrow building that would block the ocean views of his brother's building and ruin the market value. This family squabble resulted in one of the thinnest inhabitable buildings in the world, known as "The Grudge."*

*The Grudge stands on 120 square meters of land. At its widest point, it is four meters (about thirteen feet) wide, and at its smallest it is only sixty centimeters (about two feet) wide. Each floor is divided into two apartments. The kitchen is the widest room, and subsequent rooms taper down to a tiny closet at the narrowest point. Currently, The Grudge has been abandoned by everyone but a mechanic who serves as the building's caretaker and who enjoys breathtaking views of the ocean from The Grudge's windows. The building built by the other brother has become a school.*

*The Grudge can be seen as a symbol of the way family ties us together (neither brother was willing or able to simply walk away from the property arrangement) and how family estranges us from one another (The Grudge is born of the kind of spite we can surely only summon up against our relatives). It's also a symbol of mess and inefficiency, since the entire situation was initially created because decades of terrible urban planning had carved up the brothers' plots. It's located in a city that was once devastated by civil war, and thus is a symbol of both division and resilience. In Thoriya Dyer's story, "The Grudge", a man who is estranged from his family has built a fantastical version of the building, overlooking a chasm of space and time. It's a surreal story grounded in a man's need to reconcile with his family.*

———◖●◗———

The morning is normal enough, if Uthman avoids facing west. In the east, a sunrise over mountains like shards of frosted shower glass. Villages on ridges with snow on their Smart-Tile roofs. Jets to bring in the tourists, though their slipstream trails begin directly overhead, at the point where the sun marks high noon.

Beyond that, there's nothing for certain. Only the writhing possibilities of the Collision, which shows, non-chronologically, the past, the future, but almost never the present. Uthman hasn't seen a sunset over the sea since he was four years old and the family took a vacation a hemisphere to the east. He saw the red neon sun swallowed into a different ocean to the one that's behind him right now; the one that shows triremes full of dead men as often as it shows the holocausts of succeeding generations.

His boots grate on the gravel of the building site and a stick-thin figure lurks around the corner, hesitating, her high-heels wobbling on wooden formwork.

"I'm here," he calls to her. "I came early."

He's had plenty of sleep, but for some reason feels exhausted.

*Rest*, he thinks, rubbing his stubbled jaw. *I need rest.*

Rima totters, without answering, out to meet him. Maybe she's just skinny and not actually a junkie, but when you want to hate someone it's easy to find reasons. She glances at the vertical steel rails that hold private vehicles like the mismatched carriages of a war-time locomotive, scanning for his vintage hovercraft but not finding it.

He doesn't tell her that he had to sell it. And not because he saw one just like it, one time, crashed into the ocean with him, dead, inside, when he accidentally looked into the Collision. He needed the money. He's not too proud to catch a bus.

"Nice rib-bones, Rima," he says instead. They, and a smattering of bruises, are clearly visible around the edges of her flimsy, windblown shirt. She stands next to him but her eyes stay downcast. He adjusts his hat with exaggerated hand movements but he can't make her look at him. Or maybe she's trying to look up but the sheer weight of mascara is holding her lids down.

"I'm not talking to you," she says eventually, "until our lawyers come."

He laughs at that, and she joins in, nervously. He guesses they're allowed to laugh together. Until their lawyers come.

Mutt comes through the door frame, huffing like a boar that's eaten another boar for breakfast and can't breathe. His angry presence oppresses them both. There are no walls, yet, but Mutt obviously couldn't help himself. He had to come through the place where the grand entrance will be. The black-coated lawyers behind him choose the easier path, trying to keep their shiny shoes out of grey cement dust.

Reinforced concrete is what they've returned to using, now. Ever since the disaster with the sentient nanotech that was supposed to close the geological fault line. *No earthquakes ever again!* the advertising brochures had promised. *The best way to safeguard your building investment forever!*

Who could live within view of the Collision and not sign up for that? Three seconds of calm daylight on the sea. Three seconds of the moon over breaching pods of whales. Then three seconds of screams and falling towers. Lava over life-forms not yet evolved into humans. Tidal waves higher than the clouds, or aircraft carriers crushed and crumpled against a debris-strewn shore.

Here, an experiment with building in a second reality to increase real-estate square-footage led to a Collision of worlds. Yet it has always been the site of a collision of colossi, sitting square on the Dead Sea System that separates the giant Asian and African plates. Major earthquakes occur every three hundred years.

Who would build, here? With the Collision to remind them that from fiery birth to nano malfunction, this part of the world is never quiet for long? Who would try to make something last?

"Good morning, Uthman," his lawyer says in her sweet, unruffled voice. "Hello, Rima. Hello, Abd-el-Mutif."

They exchange niceties. Uthman is distracted by the feel of the Collision at his back. When their mother died and left the parcel of land to her three children in equal shares, Uthman accepted a smaller piece of the land, because his share would be closest to the view. Everyone around the world who came to stay in Saida came to gaze into the Collision, to marvel at the past or tremble in the face of all possible futures. They brought their cameras, to stretch those three seconds at a time into one thousand and five hundred frames, or they brought their soothsayers, to stare into the restless sea and work their fraudulent magic.

Only, Mutt and Rima knew before Mother's death that the edge was unstable. They knew that the place where Uthman was to have built his little pig's house of straw would collapse into the rest of the Collision, less than six months after they signed the agreement. Their surveyors and scientists had seen it.

Uthman hadn't seen. He hadn't paid for his own surveyors or scientists. He doesn't like to look at the Collision, for all that he accepted the higher value of his slice. He lives two countries away; three hours on the fast train.

"I won't sell it to you," he tells Mutt. "I don't care how much you're willing to pay."

"But Uthman," his lawyer murmurs, "what other use is it to you? You can't build an apartment block three metres wide at this end and half a metre wide at the other end. You can't prove that he swindled you, and you don't like it here, anyway. Why not take the money and go?"

*Rest,* the Collision whispers in Uthman's ears with the salt-wind voice of the sea, interfering with what the lawyer is saying. *I need rest.*

Uthman shakes his head.

"I can build," he tells his lawyer. "With an architect program and an old model fabricator, I can. Using nanotech for building above ground is not banned."

Only trying to close fault lines was against the law.

Mutt's ears, always sharp as a dog's, pick up what Uthman is saying.

"A fabricator?" he explodes. "A fabricator, when I'm building in concrete and marble? You will devalue every property in the area. The government will never approve any such application!"

"The government already has," Uthman says quietly. "I have the plans for the original block of units approved."

"Two thirds of that hideous proposed disaster is inside the Collision. Anything you poke into it won't last three seconds."

"I won't build those parts, then. But I have permission to build the parts that stand on land that's still stable, and now that there's no room for cranes or excavators, my only choice is a fabricator."

*Maybe this land isn't stable, either. What else haven't my charming siblings told me?*

Uthman resists the urge to turn his head and stare into the mesmerizing, deadly screen of the Collision that takes up half the sky.

*Rest. I need rest.*

Fabrication takes almost no time.

Uthman watches them take the extruders away from the cut-off platform of the sixth floor of his new apartment block. It is ugly, as Mutt knew it would be, seamless and beige, except for the tinted window panes, black as holes, peppering the shorn-off platforms as though an earthquake really has ripped apart an older building.

The lawyers can't approach the Collision side of the site. Uthman has left little more than a foot, barely room for a cat, between the Collision and the tall, wedge shaped excuse to block his brother's views. *The Grudge*, the newscasters are calling it.

Uthman looks down at the bald spot on Mutt's head. He has a crow's nest view of their attempts to serve him papers. Those are still required for civil proceedings. The pack of them flows around to the rear door, away from the Collision, where none of their palms against the reader result in access.

Mutt glances up. Uthman doesn't wave. He sips a tiny cup of coffee. Italian beans, his single indulgence. He hasn't shaved. Once he leaves the building, they'll ambush him with papers. He forgot his shaving kit and the extruders make only cerami-polymer and Smart-Tile. Fabricating at greater than 200 DPI can get the builders arrested. Currency is too easy to replicate and computers have never been less secure.

At the thin edge of the wedge, there's barely room for his feet. Waist-high railings practically pinch him between them. Uthman shuffles his shoes and looks at last into the Collision. He could stretch out an arm, put his hand into it, but his hand might not be safely returned to him, or it might be returned older or younger than the rest. There are fences, but people die every day trying to get new body parts.

For three seconds, below him lie the golden sands of a beach, with an island just offshore covered in ancient ruins. Three children play there, laughing. They are Uthman, Rima and Mutt. Mother, squatting on a shelf of shale, is too busy gutting the fish to notice that the children are putting the fish guts down each other's shirts.

The Collision darkens. Three seconds of sandaled warriors laying siege to the castle on the island, now connected by a stone bridge to the shore. Three seconds of summer noon stillness, a steel artificial harbour encircling the island. Then spacecraft wreckage, washed up on the beach.

A woman in an ankle-length black coat with her black braid coiled around her head, passing a screen to Mother for her to sign. The screen shows pictures of castle crenellations; no, Roman columns laid side by side; no, it's the shapes of molecules, and Mother is signing the agreement to allow the seeding of nanotech in the fault line.

Uthman tries to stumble back and comes up against the second railing. The vision feels like it's sucking at his face. He can't take his eyes away. Three seconds have passed, and the scene hasn't changed.

*I made a mistake,* he thinks in a panic. *I built over the boundary. I'm in the Collision!*

The Collision rarely shows a person their own alternate timelines. People subscribe to recording services in order to trawl for the chance of a glimpse of themselves. Uthman thought the hovercraft vision was the only one of himself or his family that he'd ever see, but now he's seen himself with his siblings on the beach, and Mother with the woman in the ankle-length coat.

There's grey in Mother's wiry red curls but her back is straight and her eyes are not yet made opaque by cataracts. How can he see her so close up? She's down on the beach, six storeys below.

"Rest," she says sternly to Uthman, and now he knows he's dead or crazy, because the Collision never makes sounds. "I need rest. Let her in, Uthman."

He twists away. Retreats indoors. Sees his silent shoes on the beige cerami-polymer. Half a metre becomes three quarters and then one metre, wide enough for the walls to fall away from his shoulders when he faces north, towards the thick end of the wedge.

There, by the narrow spiral stair, a screen advises him that the palm pressed to the outer door below is DENIED.

"Go away!" he exclaims, but the face filmed hovering curiously above the letterbox isn't Mutt's face, or Rima's. It's the woman with the black coat and the coiled black braid.

*Let her in, Uthman.*

Uthman overrides the lock. The sound of her coat swishing against close-fitting walls rises up the spiral stairwell.

"Is the owner of this building home?" she calls.

"I'm here," Uthman calls back, rubbing at his stubbled chin. She could be a killer or his future wife, a neighbour or another lawyer. He sees shapes in front of his eyes, in green and purple, as though he has stared at the sun and now must endure circles over everything.

The shapes aren't circles, though. They're alternating blocks, like battlements, and horizontal, fluted tunnels. Fallen temples, in reverse.

"I have to warn you," Uthman says to the woman, without being able to see her because he's rubbed his eyes too hard, "I think we're too close to the Collision, here. I've made a mistake. You should go."

"All the world is too close to the Collision," the woman says softly. "Unless you help me to close it."

Her name is Orla.

They breathe the fog of their loquat wine out of the space in the oversized plastic goblets that Uthman took from the aftermath of a wedding, one time.

"Can you believe that I had dreams about the Collision when I was a child, before it was made?"

Uthman squints at her. He sips. A scorpion crawls across the cracked white tiles and he stirs to crush it with a slipper. His couch smells of damp. It has cigarette-burn holes in its flower-patterned fabric. He looks at her again.

"You're not much older than me," he says.

"I was older. The Collision showed me that I was to walk into it and emerge, young again. When I went in, I was a painter. An artist. When I came out, I was an engineer, with all the knowledge that I needed. And still, I grew old before I could solve it. I made mistakes. I thought fusing the geologic fault lines would close the Collision, but I failed, and so I had to go in a second time for the gift of a third lifespan."

Uthman shivers and says nothing.

"You don't seem shocked. You must think I am lying. All other claims of visions and powers granted by the Collision have been proven false. You think I am like those attention seekers."

He pours more wine and doesn't disclose that the Collision has shown him things, too.

"I don't think that," he says. "I saw you on the beach. Where you tried to close the fault."

She shakes her head.

"I do not know which timeline that was," she murmurs. "I barely know which timeline I am in. The Collision has shown me myself, failing again and again. It tries to teach me but I am a slow learner. It wants to close."

"It wants to close? It doesn't want anything. It just is."

She empties the goblet in a single, long swallow.

"It wants to close," she says vehemently. "Human activity disturbs it. When it has opened before, and become self-aware, it has opened in space, or on dead planets, where the variations are manageable. There, the variations are few. Here, the variations are inexhaustible. The Collision is exhausted. That is why it is unstable. That is why it grows."

*Rest. I need rest.*

"Woman," Uthman says, stifling the urge to laugh hysterically. "If your destiny is failure and my destiny is death, what's the use of us talking together?"

"Who says your destiny is death?"

Uthman's hand on the stolen plastic rubbish trembles as he remembers his face covered in blood. The three awful seconds of the hovercraft vision replays in his mind. He's inside the cabin with a head wound from the impact. No, he's outside the craft and Mutt is the driver and the accident is no accident. No, the hovercraft is parked nearby and a building has fallen on him. It's an earthquake. It's the Collision, widening.

It's the end.

"Stop doing that," he cries, dropping the drink. "I sold it! It's gone."

"I'm not doing anything," Orla protests.

"What are you doing here?"

"You invited me to your house. We took the train, together, from the Grudge at the Collision's edge to this unit where you live."

"No, I mean why did you come to The Grudge?"

"I had to talk to you. I've never seen the version with you, before. The Collision showed me your brother signing the consent, or your sister, but never you. Maybe that's because it ends if I choose you."

"What consent?"

She holds out her screen and it shows pictures of castle crenellations. No, Roman columns laid side by side. No, it's the shapes of molecules, the graphic header on an agreement to allow the seeding of nanotech in the Collision. The absolution of risk. The understanding of unpredictable consequences.

Uthman ignores the orange stain spreading on the filthy couch.

"How can my consent mean anything? It's the government that has to approve this sort of thing and they don't want the Collision closed. They've never made so much money from tourism before. Not even the threat of death can keep people away."

"It's your land," Orla says. "The law is clear. You can do what you want with nanotech on your land, as long as it doesn't spread underground, and I have no intention of putting it in the ground. That railing where you stood will do just fine."

"Are you sure that it wants to die? Are you sure you're helping it and not harming it? What if you're making it angry and that's why it's unstable? What if it's going to kill me for helping you?"

Orla draws herself up stiffly, eyes cold.

"Have you no care for anyone else in this world? Friends? Family?"

"No," he says at once. "To hell with them."

"The Collision isn't hell. Not exactly. But it's close."

"I don't care."

"Would you have done it to him, if your positions were reversed? If you knew that the land would eventually be useless, but Abd-el-Mutif did not? Would you lure him in, would you give him the best land, the best position, the best view?"

"Of course not!"

"Yet you were willing to take it. You don't live there. You don't like it. Looking at it makes you shit your pants but you won't sell it."

"Look at me. Look where I am living." He gestures furiously at the bullet holes in the broken walls from decades-old, abandoned conflicts, the torn posters showing beaches that cannot be seen, now, for longer than three seconds at a time, which paper over pits in the beige cerami-polymer. He cannot afford repairs. He cannot afford better. "They never visit me. It shames them to look at this, when they're used to granite and gold leaf. Well, let them look at The Grudge from their fancy mansions. Let them think of me when their tenants complain that all they can see is the sky."

"Your mother signed because she wanted you three to be safe. Her father told her stories about the ground coming alive and heaving, terracotta pots shooting from apartment windows like a clay-pigeon trap's revenge. It wasn't just you that she wanted to protect. She wanted Rima to be safe, and Abd-el-Mutif."

"My mother never signed anything!"

"Not in this timeline. You're right. I don't think I met her, in this one."

Uthman sucks air in through flared nostrils. Mother wanted to protect Mutt and Rima? She should have drowned them in a well at birth! If only she was alive to see how Mutt shovels eggs into his face like a reverse farm full of battery hens, or how Rima simpers for her bald and impotent parole officer so he won't ask her for a urine sample to prove that she's clean!

"Mothers will forgive anything," he says.

"Even the end of the world? Are you sure about that?"

Angrily, he wipes his hands on his jeans. Then he stops caring about smearing her screen and presses his palm to the contract. It is signed.

"You had better be right this time, woman."

"I am right," Orla says perfunctorily. "This time, this place, I will not fail."

Uthman stands uneasily on the footpath, hands in his pockets.

He doesn't want to be inside the building while Orla does what she has to do, but he can't make himself walk back to the train station, either. Nearby, a cluster of Americans consults a map of the Old City, marveling that the sea-castle which was only a weathered ruin before the Collision opened can now be seen swarming with Crusader knights or being built, block by block, by the bare hands of brown slaves.

Sometimes the castle stands in a future where it floats on a cloud. Sometimes it is blown apart by cannon fire before it is even finished being built, in a world where science comes to the margins before it reaches this, the center. In the three-second dark, the island is a refuge for sea-turtles laying eggs. In the three-second day, it is a nuclear test site.

Then it all goes grey.

Uthman blinks.

He rubs his eyes to make the green and purple shapes, like battlements, go away. Then he walks forward. The woman with the long, black coat and coiled braid waits to meet him by the parked personal hovercraft. He's selling it to her. The Grudge, which he built to get revenge on his brother, Abd-el-Mutif, is too narrow to fit a private vehicle. This woman, an art gallery curator, has brought the contract of sale.

"It passed the performance tests?" he asks, taking the screen from her hand and flicking through the pages.

"Like it was brand new," she answers, smiling.

Uthman puts his palm to the screen. The hovercraft is hers, now. The money is transferred quietly to his account. He'll need it, because he is moving to the top floor of the wedge-shaped building, displacing one of his best customers, but he's had enough of living away from the sea. Some of his best memories are of growing up by the beach.

He looks up, across the four lane highway and out over the water, at the castle on the island surrounded by the cranes and loaders of the working port. For a moment, it seems like the alternating-block silhouette of the battlements is being made whole, zipping together with another, identical, upside-down castle.

Laughing, he turns to see his sister, Rima, crossing the street with her two big-eyed, waif-like children.

"So," she says, not meeting his eyes. "We're going to be neighbors."

The woman with the coat gets into the hovercraft and drives away, waving absently as she enters the heavy traffic on the noisy major road.

"Looks like it," Uthman answers, fishing in his pockets for chiclets and handing them out to the kids without asking.

"Mutt still hates you," she says.

"But not you?"

"Well, it's true I don't get to see the water from my window. But the traffic is pretty noisy and your building reflects and blocks a lot of it. My kids can get a peaceful night's sleep."

"Well. That's good."

Rima suddenly seizes the leather of his sleeve.

"Uthman, I'm so sorry. Yes, I sort of knew the highway was going to take away most of your land, but I wasn't paying attention, really. You know I had other problems to deal with at the time."

Uthman sighs.

"Sure. I know."

"So." At last, she lifts her gaze to his. "Maybe we could go for a walk along the beach. The café has good *knefeh*."

Uthman dreams of a confusing movie he's never seen.

The editing is terrible. It changes every three seconds or so. Sometimes it's night and sometimes it's day, but the same thing always seems to happen: A man in jeans and a leather jacket gets hit and killed by a red hovercraft.

Sometimes a woman with a braid wrapped around her head gets out and tries to help him but the man dies anyway. Mostly they're on land, on a street or the narrow sandy swathe of the beach. Sometimes they're on an island and occasionally there's no island at all, only the sea, and the man is swimming and the driver of the hovercraft just doesn't see him.

When she does see him, she swerves away, only for the swell or a bystander or an earthquake to drag him into her path.

But these are stitched up memories, mere elaborations of a mind finally at rest, and Uthman only half-remembers them when he wakes.

# — SANTA CRUZ: A TRUE STORY —
## Andy Duncan

*Everyone in California knows three things about Santa Cruz: it's very beautiful, it's very fun, and it's very weird. Santa Cruz attracts hippies, tourists, ghost stories, college students, vortexes, and coincidences. To go to Santa Cruz to enter a slightly parallel universe where everything is just slightly askew and perfectly delightful.*

*Santa Cruz is a beach town in Northern California. Its first residents were the Ohlone people, who lived in small villages as hunters, fisher, and gatherers. The Spanish were interested in the area, and founded a series of missions along the coastline. The Spanish mission system, which introduced diseases and forced the Ohlone to live and work in the missions, virtually destroyed the Ohlone culture. In the 1820s, Mexico gained independence from Spain and assumed control of Santa Cruz. Santa Cruz became an American city in 1850, after the Mexican-American War.*

*Santa Cruz is, allegedly, home to a multitude of ghosts and supernatural anomalies. Brookdale Lodge is said to be haunted by a little girl who died there. Arana Gulch is haunted by a farmer who was shot and killed in the gulch one night. A White Lady, the ghost of an abused bride, roams the streets of Santa Cruz at night, and the Rispon Mansion is said to house at least three ghosts (a woman, a man, and a dog). The Mystery Spot is a cabin in which the laws of physics seem to be reversed. Tourists visit the site every year to witness bizarre illusions and distortions involving gravity and perspective. Explanations for the Mystery Spot range from the alleged presence of an alien spacecraft buried under the cabin, to a simple optical illusion stemming from the fact that the cabin is tilted.*

*With all the paranormal activity, it's no surprise that Any Duncan's visit to Santa Cruz was a little unusual. If there's one thing you can expect from Santa Cruz, it's that nothing will happen quite as you suspect.*

I n summer 2013, during a business trip to Southern California, I decided to drive my rental car past Los Angeles to visit friends to the north. The farthest I got was my old classmate Rob, who met me for dinner in his adopted hometown of Santa Cruz.

Though we'd kept in touch, Rob and I hadn't been in one another's company for 19 years. We were pleased to find one another exactly the same, or close enough. Rob was, and is, a mystic. He has worked on fishing boats and in slaughterhouses, lived in communes, ingested many mind-expanding substances, religions, philosophies. His is a life of meditative inquiry. You might call him a seeker.

After we roamed one of Rob's favorite landscapes, Henry Cowell Redwoods State Park, we enjoyed a long, leisurely, drunken dinner in the outdoor garden of The Crepe Place on Soquel Avenue, as Rob talked mostly about the strange forces that kept him tied to Santa Cruz.

He had moved there years before for seasonal work, but had stayed on, for reasons hard to explain to the Chamber of Commerce. Santa Cruz, Rob explained, was a place of mystery. Not in the sense of the Mystery Spot, that famous local tourist trap. No, from the moment he took up residence there, Santa Cruz had announced itself to Rob as a place vibrating with unique energies. It was haunted, of course (that went without saying), but it was on Rob's wavelength, somehow. Amazing coincidences, Jungian synchronicities, unlikely serendipities, tugged at his sleeve daily in Santa Cruz. Who knew the reason? A Holy Cross, certainly, was inherent in the name, but what more intractable powers had that old Franciscan tasted, back in 1769, in that "good arroyo of running water", worth naming in his diary? What explanation would have been offered by the Ohlone people, who were there when the Spanish arrived? Ley lines, sacred groves, thin places in the multiverse, some subterranean shard of the ancient Atlantean power source—who could say? Whatever the explanation, Rob said, the effects were real, and would be noticeable even to a hoary old skeptic like me…if I just hung around long enough.

"Sounds as if you're in the right place, all right," I blandly told him, mentally crossing off stops on my next-day itinerary. The coastal highway to San Simeon, then inland to Lompoc, and a leg of lamb with Melissa and her family.

By this time we had left the restaurant, it was late at night, and the moon was overhead. It looked full to me, but I realize now, checking the records, that all this happened Friday, June 21, actually two nights before the full in Santa Cruz. Still, the night was very bright, unnervingly so. I drove Rob back in my air-conditioned Yaris to the parking lot north of town where he had left his battered pickup truck.

As Rob and I walked across the dark, nearly empty parking lot, approaching his ancient vehicle that looked as though it had survived many a stoning, and talked about everything and nothing, a patch of darkness in our path rose up, resolved itself, took on form.

While we wondered what we were looking at, what we were approaching, we heard a woman whimpering and sniffling. She was on her hands and knees in front of us, gathering the spilled contents of her purse. No car was near, and the lot otherwise was deserted.

"Are you OK, ma'am?" I asked. I am ashamed to say that I consciously dropped my voice a register, trying to sound less like myself and more like Sam Elliott.

"Son of a bitch knocked me down," she said. She lurched to her feet and wavered, unsteady. In her heels, she was nearly as tall as me, and she wore a night-on-the-town dress, but we could see nothing of her face.

"Do you need help, ma'am? Should we call the police?"

"Just want to go home," she said, slurring her words: *Jus' wan' g'home*. She began to walk away, toward the trees at the far edge of the lot.

"Do you have a car?" I asked, not liking the idea of her driving anywhere.

"Got no car," she replied. "Walking. Just over there." She didn't point, but waved her arm toward the dark woods.

The moment I began to write about this, I began to question the details, my own memory. That's why I looked up the full moon, a page ago. As I recall that conversation in the parking lot, beneath a *nearly* full moon, the woman and I are doing all the talking. Yet some of this questioning must have been done by Rob, who certainly did not stand there mute. He's a talkative guy. Probably I attribute our side of the conversation only to me out of egotism, or to assume the blame for the folly that immediately ensued, when in my memory I said:

"Don't worry, ma'am. I'll drive you home, and my friend will follow us."

Now, little about that was smart. This was a complete stranger, of only a few seconds' acquaintance, clearly drunk, and I was inviting her into my car, where not only would I be at her mercy—if she were armed, or if she were to attack me bare-handed at close quarters—but where *she* would be at *my* mercy, too. Suppose, in her hazy state, she decided that I had abducted her, assaulted her? And what of the absent "son of a bitch"? How far away was he, really? How violently might he react, upon returning to the lot to find "his" woman climbing into a strange man's car? Or was the whole damsel-in-distress routine a setup for blackmail, or worse? Was he watching us right now, through a high-powered camera lens, or night-vision goggles?

In other words, kids, don't try this at home.

But all these concerns I thought of, with growing trepidation, only once she was in my car. Opening the door for her and gesturing her in, rather grandly, was a total impulse, done with no thought whatsoever. There would be more of that, later.

She got in with no fuss, no argument, and in the brief dome light I saw that her left knee was scraped and bleeding. Her arms and shoulders were bare. She was blonde and lean and looked muscular; I could picture her on a tennis court or golf course. She had a long face and bad teeth. That's all I registered as I hastened to lock the doors, buckle up and drive out of there. She needed no help buckling up, thank goodness.

Rob was right behind me as our two-vehicle caravan left the parking lot, turning right onto the highway. Moments later, at the first cross street, the woman told me to turn right again. The moment I turned off the highway, I lost Rob.

The highway was visible in my rear mirror only for a few yards, before my passenger had me turn again. In those few moments that the highway was visible to me, and my taillights visible from the highway, no Rob. How could he have missed me? He was only a few yards behind, on a deserted street. It was as if he had driven into a thin place in the cosmos, and been lost to the world. Or maybe he was thinking the same thing, at this moment, of me.

If I were to revisit that neighborhood now, by day, it might look utterly ordinary: cozy, compact, unthreatening. But that night, all my senses on high alert, it was like driving through the Thieves' District of Lankhmar. The streets were narrow, little more than alleys, and inert automobiles of all eras and states of disrepair jumbled the shoulders. Overgrown hedges and trees raked my car on both sides. The houses of clapboard and shingle were narrow and vertical, many on pilings as along an ocean or riverside, and each seemed somehow aslant, leaning into one another and looming over my car and slumping into the alleys as if embarrassed by their own decay. Our route was level enough, but I was conscious of forested mountainsides now on my left, now on my right, each clustered with houses that clung for purchase on chicken legs. I remember no streetlights, no other moving vehicles, only the glow of small, feral eyes as I turned corner after corner at my passenger's monotone directions: left, right, right, left, left.

I had no confidence in my navigator. She kept up a murmuring monologue about the son of a bitch who knocked her down, who left her in the parking lot, who thought he knew so goddamn much, but no more information was forthcoming beyond these well-worn cycles. She seemed heedless of where I was taking her, and I soon realized that she gave me a turn instruction only when I asked for one. She then would interrupt herself instantly, only to say "left" or "right," without looking at anything, then return to the topic of the good-for-nothing son of a bitch who knew so goddamn much. I was sure she was making up the directions as she went along.

Finally I braked just before running head-on into a railroad-tie wall that marked the end of cul-de-sac. I looked at the identical crazy houses to either side. Something made a dash for the underbrush, and a garbage can clattered in sympathy.

"Is one of these your house, ma'am?" I asked.

She flapped her free hand, as if shooing a fly. "No, mine's over on the other street somewhere." Her non-free hand reached for me. "You're cute," she said.

I half-rose in my seat, hackles on end like a cartoon cat's. "Oh, no, ma'am," I said. "That's not why we're out here. I'm taking you home, and that's all. Either you tell me where that is, or you'll have to get out of this car, right now."

How I would enforce this gallant threat, I had no idea and have none today. In response she laughed, deeply and fully. "You're cute," she repeated. "All right, back up. It's the next street over." Her finger-nails scuttled across her passenger-side window, click click click. She sounded unimpressed by my chivalry. Probably she had heard such claims before.

As I backed up the car, she continued addressing her remarks to me, as if in her mind I now had displaced the previous son of a bitch. "I like the way you talk," she said, stretching her vowels in imitation. "Where are you from?"

"South Carolina, originally," I said, not adding that everyone in South Carolina marvels at my accent, too.

"South Carolina," she drawled, imitating me again. "Oh, my God, South Carolina. I like the way you talk." This was her new speech cycle, repeated with small variations during the next few minutes.

Her street actually was three-and-a-half streets over, by my count, but presently she had me stop, and to my great relief she unbuckled without a fuss and opened her door. She got out, swayed a bit, then leaned in to grab her purse, the cleavage of her dress gaping. "Let me shake your hand," she said, still leaning in, and I did. Hers was a strong, decisive, businesslike handshake, a formal goodbye. In the dome light she seemed both older and younger than I had envisioned. "You've been very sweet," she said, "and I appreciate it. Tell me your name, honey?"

I was flustered into honesty. "My name's Andy," I said.

And then something remarkable happened.

Have you seen the movie *Junebug*? If you have, you'll remember that Amy Adams plays Ashley, a naïve small-town North Carolinian who has fantasized her whole life about Japan. She meets a sophisticated woman, Madeleine, played by Embeth Davidtz, a visitor from the big city, who is only half paying attention to this local girl who clearly idolizes her. Ashley innocently mentions Japan, whereupon Madeleine replies, as an over-the-shoulder aside, that she grew up in Japan. At that moment, the camera focuses on Amy Adams's face, as Ashley tries to process this information. Finally she murmurs, "You did *not*."

When I said "Andy," that night in Santa Cruz, the play of expressions across that woman's face was the same as that on Amy Adams's face in that scene. Her eyes widened and seemed to recede into her head. The smile and frown lines on her face smoothed away. Her mouth dropped open. Even her hair seemed no longer lank and stringy; it now waved around her much-younger face in an improbably localized breeze. And in the very same throaty voice with which Amy Adams said, "You did *not*," this woman said, "It is *not*."

"Yes, ma'am," I said. "That's my name." I am ashamed, now, to realize I did not ask hers.

"You are shitting me," she said.

"No, ma'am," I said. "Is something wrong?"

She chuckled and said, "Just look at this." She turned and sat in the passenger's seat, facing out, away from me. Gathering her hair out of the way, she unfastened the clasp of her dress and unzipped, shrugging forward until her shoulders were bare. A single oblong tattoo covered the width of her back, across both shoulder blades. It was a single four-letter name in Gothic letters against an ornate backdrop of trellised roses:

ANDY

She carried on her back, every waking moment, my name.

"Well, how about that," I said, lapsing into my late father-in-law's favorite thing to say when he had nothing to say.

"Yeah, ain't that the shit?" the woman said, perhaps reciting her own stock family response. She straightened her dress, said, "Good night, hon," got out of the car and closed the door behind her. I lunged over to immediately lock it and stayed in position, watching her walk to her front door, find her key with minimal fuss, walk in and close the door behind her. She never looked back.

Now my challenge was finding my way *out* of this maze. But serendipity having ridden along this far, I decided to trust it a little longer. "I'll make random turns," I said aloud, "and assume it'll come out OK." I might as well have said, "Trust in the Force, Luke," but no matter. I turned around, made three unthinking turns—left, right, left—and there was the highway, right in front of me. I had taken twenty minutes to drive into that neighborhood, less than a minute to drive out. That is probably impossible, but it happened.

And at the stop sign, wondering where Rob was (because my phone had no signal, of course), I decided to turn right, on the assumption that Rob awaited me in his truck just the other side of that tall hedge. And when I passed the hedge –

But you're way ahead of me, I see.

I pulled alongside Rob's truck as he rolled down his window. "What happened, man?" he cried. "Where have you been?"

"I'll tell you at your place," I said. "Just lead the way."

His place turned out not actually to be in Santa Cruz, not even in the old logging town of Felton to the north, but in the countryside beyond that, at the top of a box canyon, and it was less a house than a repurposed shed in a redwood grove. But in front of Rob's iron cookstove and his homemade motherboard, I told him the whole detailed story I just have told you.

He indicated throughout no concerns, no surprise. Fingers laced across his belly, eyes half-lidded, he only nodded thoughtfully, radiating peace and contentment.

When I was done, he spread his hands in blessing and said: "I rest my case, man. That shit happens in Santa Cruz *all the time*."

That's the story, as I've told it to only a few people since. Prodded by friends, I now am writing it down, though with some hesitation. As all writers know, writing things down, then typing them out, makes them more real, more consequential.

In the middle of writing this, feeling weirded out, I put down my notebook and picked up my current pleasure reading, Volume Two of Bill Patterson's Robert A. Heinlein biography. The first sentence I glanced at led me to a footnote that cited the Heinlein archives...at UC-Santa Cruz.

Then my email pinged, with a note from my friend Karen, who lives in...Santa Cruz.

Unnerved, I reached for a sack of cookies. My mother-in-law bought them, for this family beach trip I'm on. I wasn't with her when she bought them. They are oatmeal-raisin cookies, very tasty. They are a trademarked flavor of Pepperidge Farm Soft Baked cookies. The package says, "Our Santa Cruz cookie is a popular destination.... You're going to love it here!"

Writing things down makes them more real, more consequential. And I now know, as I did not know when I sat down, that a woman who carries my name on her back will cross my path again, if ever I return to Santa Cruz.

# — AND THE TREES WERE HAPPY —
## Scott Edelman

*Scott Edelman's story "And the Trees Were Happy" was inspired by Shel Silverstein's book The Giving Tree. In The Giving Tree, an apple tree loves a boy. As a child, The Boy's needs are simple. He wants to swing from the tree's branches and eat her apples, and she is happy to oblige. As he grows, his desires become more complex. He wants money, so the tree gives him all of her apples to sell. He wants a house, so the tree offers her branches for lumber. He wants a boat, so the tree offers her trunk. As an old man, the boy returns to the tree, wanting a place to rest. He sits on the tree's stump, "And the tree was happy."*

*The Giving Tree has been analyzed in many ways. Some see the story as a shining example of unconditional love. Others see the boy as abusive. Some view the story as a religious allegory, some as an environmental message, and others as a metaphor for relationships between mothers and children. Some people adore The Giving Tree and others hate it. Silverstein refused to elaborate on the message behind the book. "It's just a relationship between two people. One gives and one takes," he said.*

*In Edelman's story, an old man returns to the tree he once loved and is greeted with a response he does not expect. The tree has some harsh truths for the old man, but the love between them remains strong.*

**T**he old man slowly and carefully lowered himself onto the stump—for, after all, everything he did these days had to be done slowly and carefully—and as the ancient wood pressed against his bony flesh, he was surprised by the surge of emotions that brought on a sudden welling of tears. He looked up through wet eyes at the empty air where a tree had at one time towered above him, and recalled how he had once swung effortlessly through branches which, if he had not cut them down so long ago, would now have shielded him from an oppressive sun.

The twinge of pain that traveled through his hips as he connected with the stump surprised him. It was something he would never have imagined, back when he was a young boy, waited in his future.

And yet somehow, as he settled in, he found comfort there, as if it had been carved for him alone. The walk through the orchard had been longer than he'd remembered it being, and his need to sit was overwhelming. But then, most things these days were longer than he remembered. Longer, more difficult, and often filled with an almost unendurable sadness.

Still, he had managed to endure. And unexpectedly, after years—decades actually—return.

He felt a bit foolish to have done so, though, even as he knew the return had recently become inevitable. He'd been haunted lately by ancient memories he found he could not elude, and drawn by them to this orchard close to his childhood home. Drawn, more specifically, to this tree, or the remnant of same, at the site of which he had passed so many of his life's most important moments.

Many of his memories of this place were cloudy now, and as he sought them out, he suspected, too, that they were surely muddled by an old man's brain. As a boy, he had spoken to the tree, treated it as a friend, of that he was certain, and he saw nothing wrong with that, for that is what boys, what children, do. But—and here is where he did not believe what he remembered—had the tree really spoken back? Surely that was not possible. He assumed this was only the hot sun inserting those memories into his mind. Because...what else could it be?

He should have remembered to wear a hat. Or should, at least, have brought along some water. For he was thirsty, a thirst which resurrected on his tongue the taste of the apples which had once grown above him, and which had quenched his thirst like nothing since.

But those apples were gone now, first to be sold for money so he could buy toys, then because he needed the branches which bore them to build a house, and finally due to his hewing of wood for a boat. And now all those things were gone as well...money, house, boat...plus the wife and child those first possessions had gotten him.

The wife who would have reminded him about the hat. The child who would have trailed after him to gently place a bottle of water in his hand.

No, now he had nothing, nothing save the clothes on his back and the elusive memories which had brought him here.

The memory of the stump on which he sat. The memory of what it had once been. The memory of what *he* had once been.

If only he could taste an apple again! If only he could go back. He would do anything for that. But he could think of nothing which could be done. Because there was nothing which *could* be done. The orchard's other trees, the other apples, they were not like this tree, those apples.

Which made his return…pointless.

As he wondered why he had bothered, why his childhood had intruded on his life once more in a way he could no longer reject, he noticed that the sun had dropped behind the orchard's closest row of trees, the nearby branches casting a shadow across his face.

How odd. How could so much time could have passed, high noon transforming into those elusive moments before dusk, without him being aware of it?

But as he looked into the shade-filled gathering of the trees, he quickly forgot that, for he could make out an abundant display of heavy apples tugging at their branches, a thing he'd somehow over-looked before. The weight of them was a living thing calling him, and he wondered…if he rose, if he reached out his hand to pluck one, if he held it to his lips, touched it to his tongue…would it be as sweet as memory? Could anything ever be?

He knew he had to try. He stood, and took a step forward toward them, but then stumbled—for his rear foot had caught under one of the stump's exposed roots.

He fell to the ground, a pain shooting sharply up his leg. Had he broken an ankle? Based on the ache that remained, it felt as if he had, but he'd endured so many pains in recent years, he couldn't be entirely sure. He wiggled his foot, which seemed trapped where it had become wedged between the root and the stump, and no matter how hard he tried, could not pull it free.

"How could you do this to me?" he almost said aloud to the stump, feeling betrayed by a thing which he knew could not possibly have the sentience to betray him, but caught himself, silenced himself, before he acted even more foolishly than he already had by coming there. This was no one's fault but his own. And for whatever reason—a momentary distraction, the clumsiness of his gait, which over the years had turned into more of a shuffle—his foot was stuck.

Out of breath, and unable to pull loose his twisted foot, he lay on his back and looked up at the darkening sky. He wondered how many hours, how many days, it would be before anyone wandered by this remote place who could help, and what they would think of the silly old man when they found him.

Slowly, a branch from the nearest tree grew nearer above him, lengthening into his field of vision, a lone apple at its tip pushing forward to hang tantalizingly close. The fruit pulsed with possibility, and he held out a hand, but could not reach it. The more he stretched, the more tightly the root squeezed around his foot, preventing him from closing the infuriating gap.

"Please," said the old man. "Please let me have just one more apple."

As if in response, the branch above him trembled. As if in response, the root beneath him squeezed. And then the tree which had grown toward him impossibly fast to tease him with its tempting fruit spoke, its words all around him, its words *in* him.

"Do not worry," said the tree, though as its words filled his mind, the man knew it was speaking, not just for itself, but on behalf of the entire orchard. "The fruit will be yours. If you truly want it, that is."

"I do," said the man, embarrassed by his greed and glad no one else was there to hear the naked desire quivering in his voice. "But I can't quite reach it. My foot, you see. It's become stuck."

"We know," said the tree. "But it hasn't *just* become stuck. It's become trapped. *You've* become trapped. There has always been a part of us that loved you too much. It loved you too much then. It loves you too much now. It wants to stop you from eating the apple that would let you see things clearly. Even now, even after all you have done, it wants to keep giving. But now it's time for a giving of an entirely different kind."

The branch shook, its leaves rustling like the wind from another time, and the dangling apple danced seductively at the end of its stem. For a few agonizing moments, it looked as if the stem would hold, and the man dared not breathe, but then the fruit broke free and landed with a plop in his hungry palm.

He held it to his nose, the aroma dizzying. As he did so, he could feel the root pulse against his ankle, and he knew it was urging him to drop the apple. At the same time, he could almost hear it whisper. But whatever it was trying to say was unimportant. He was beyond convincing.

He bit roughly, and as his teeth broke the skin of the fruit and the moist flesh touched his tongue, his foot was released.

And he was young again.

And so was the tree on whose stump he'd been sitting.

Its trunk thrust high above him, leaping for the sky. Its branches bent to offer shade and extend an invitation.

He accepted that invitation. Laughing, he shinnied up the trunk until he could touch the lowest branch. Then he leapt, and swung, and crouched atop it. He jeered the ground so far below, dared gravity to have its way with him, but he knew it could not, for wasn't he a boy?

He gathered leaves as he had in days past and once more wove himself a crown so he could declare himself king of the forest. Ruler of all he surveyed, he swung from branch to branch until he tired, and then had his fill of the sweetest apples in the world before settling in the shade for a nap.

When he woke, he was…older. A teenager, perhaps? He had grown so old in the world outside this vision that he could no longer gauge the age of the young, not even when he was the one who was young. And as he filled a basket with apples so he could carry them away and sell them to buy things he believed would bring him fun, it was as if he was both doing and observing, and he saw more than he'd experienced when he'd lived through it the first time. Now he could see that the tree was not as happy as it had claimed to be at his taking. No, it was sad, for it had meant the apples to be his alone. He saw that now, and it made him sad to have made it sad. But it was too late to change that. It was too late to change anything.

And then more time passed in the living of a life he'd moved through blindly the first time around, and the tree offered him first its branches, and later its trunk as well, so he could build things and be happy. And he had been happy (or so he'd thought), and the tree had been happy (or so he'd thought as well), only…it was not. It had never been. It wept silently as he'd removed its limbs, not wanting him to see its pain, and he hadn't, so desperate was he for the things he thought he would die if he did not have.

This time, he winced with each cut. This time, every swing of the axe, every slice of the saw, cut into his own heart as well. But again, he could not change what this vision let him see. The doing of it was done.

And then, a final vision—that day he'd returned after a long absence to sit on the stump for the first and only time up until now, that moment of rest being the only gift the tree had left to give.

But he did not stay for long. He could not. Perhaps, somewhere deep inside and unacknowledged, he knew what he had done, what he did not want to face, so he left to abandon and forget.

And with that forgetting caused the thing that loved him most the greatest pain of all. Until dreams and memories and the call of an angry orchard drew him back.

"I didn't know," he whimpered as he returned to the reality of what was left of his life. "I didn't realize. I thought—"

"What was it that you thought?" said the tree, on behalf of all trees.

"I thought," he said, pressing his back against the stump which he had made. "I thought that's what love was."

"And yet, you are alone," said the trees.

"And yet, I am here," said the man.

"And you expect your presence, a presence which would not have occurred without our call, to be enough? You expect your return to make up for what you have done? How would you like it if we were to make of you what you have made of part of us?"

The man's mind filled with an image of grasping branches tearing his limbs from his body one by one, until what remained was as helpless as the stump on which he'd sat. He gasped, but did not object. Because he was weary, and now knew far too well the revealed truth which he had long fought to keep hidden.

"It would be no more and no less than what I deserve," he said.

"Then," said the orchard. "So shall it be."

Other branches stretched out to fill the sky, joining the one which had offered him the apple. They reached for his arms and legs, and as he raised his head to them, as he held his arms wide, he was ready.

But then the earth around the stump behind him rumbled, and what remained of the tree rose out of the ground, thrust upward by its roots. It walked clumsily on those wooden legs until it covered the man's body with its bulk, shielding him from harm. And in his mind, the man could make out the whisper he'd thought he'd heard before, but had been unable to decipher.

"Come, boy," it said as he curled beneath it.

The branches sought him out, but the stump scrambled this way and that, repeatedly blocking them.

"You would do this?" said the trees in conversation with themselves, pausing the attack. "After all that has been done to us?"

"I would," said the stump.

"But you have loved too much," said the trees. "You know that. And you have loved wrongly."

"If I have loved wrongly," said the stump. "At least I have loved. At least *we* have loved."

The branches trembled slightly, their leaves like sighs, and then, after a pause during which the man did not know what decision he truly wanted the trees to make, they retreated.

The stump crawled away and exposed him to a sun that was low in the sky, but no longer hidden, then settled into the earth once more.

And the man rose shakily to his feet, his joints cracking, his chest pained.

He moved closer to the stump, hoping to sit there one more time, but could not reach it, and fell to his knees a few footsteps short. He reached out to rest his hands where he had once so callously rested his ax.

"I am very tired," he said, gasping for breath. "And very sorry."

"Well," said the tree, once again as tall and proud as when the man, then a boy, had first run through the orchard and spotted it in the distance. "Lay yourself down and rest."

"I will," said the boy. He stretched out beneath the magical tangle of branches, placing his head softly on a moss-covered root.

As he closed his eyes, he dreamed he was king of the forest.

And then he dreamed no more.

And the trees were happy.

# — WELL OF TRANQUILITY —
## Steven H Silver

*"Well of Tranquility", by Steven H Silver, is set at G'ndevank Monastery. The monastery is very old. Its central building, the church of St. Stepanos, dates back to 936. In 1604 much of the monastery was destroyed, but it was rebuilt in 1691, this time with high walls. Protected by its walls and riddled with underground rooms and passages, the monastery endures through the turbulent history of Armenia.*

*Christianity came early to Armenia—in fact, it became the first officially Christian state in 301. Long before Christianity came to Armenia, a complex and frequently shifting mythology existed. In this tradition, Vahagn the Dragon Reaper ruled, along with his lover, Astghik. Astghik was the goddess of fertility, love, and water. One legend about Astghik tells of her spreading love throughout Armenia by sprinkling rose water everywhere she went. The festival of Vartavar is still celebrated throughout Armenia in the summer. It's a playful, riotous celebration during which people splash each other with water in honor of the goddess.*

*Christianity has a long tradition of co-opting pagan festivals and turning them into Christian ones. Rather than attempt to stamp out the festival of Vartavar, the Church tried to claim it as their own. According to Christian tradition, Noah ordered his sons to spill water on each other in remembrance of the Flood. The holiday is known as the Feast of Transfiguration, and the holiday commemorates Christ's appearance to his disciples on Mount Tabor. But people still remember the Goddess Astghik and her healing rose water. The water dumped on you from your neighbor's balcony during Vartavar is startling, refreshing, healing—and still fun, even after centuries.*

⎯⎯⎯⸻●⸺⎯⎯⎯

**A**bove the Armenian mountain village of Gndevaz, there is a monastery that was founded in the tenth century. Sprouting from this monastery, like a tumor, is a small room that predates the rest of G'ndevank monastery by an unknown number of centuries. Small and dark, this room was accessible only to a few select monks throughout the ages. Men the Abbot felt could withstand the utter sensation of peace that overcame those who spent any amount of time in the cell.

I was tending the monastery's vineyard with several other brothers when Brother Onik came to tell me that Abbot Mesrop needed to speak to me immediately. We hurried down the mountain, Brother Onik, whose young feet were much more sure than my own, leading the way and me trying to keep up as he found some invisible path through the weeds and scarp.

Brother Onik guided me to the postern gate and held it open for me before we hurried through the narrow, ancient stone hallways that made up the monastery. A place of worship and meditation, G'ndavank was seemingly built to withstand a siege by the Byzants and the Seljuks. While both those tribes had over run Gndevaz in their time, the city, and the monastery, still stood while the Byzants and Seljuks were mere memories the old women in town used to frighten children with.

Abbot Mesrop sat in his office behind a massive wooden desk that seemed as much a part of the monastery as the stone walls, but which couldn't have been more than fifty years old, younger, in fact, than the Abbot, who had ruled the monastery since the time of the great purges, and now Abbot Mesrop and G'ndevank were still standing, while the Stalinists were as much the dead past as the Seljuks. I stood in silence, waiting for the Holy Father to look up and acknowledge me. He took his time finishing writing something with the old-fashioned fountain pen he always used, carefully blotted the page, and looked up at me. "Brother Sevak," he said in his deep voice that brought importance to even the most trivial utterance.

"Holy Father," I replied, practically a ritual, as was everything that happened within the ancient stone walls.

"I have been monitoring your progress for many years," he began. With only a score of monks on the grounds of the monastery that once housed more than 100, this was no great feat, but I bowed my head in humility and understanding.

"I've watched you interact the other brothers. Quietly, nothing overt, nothing obvious. They see you as a leader even if you don't see yourself that way. Our Lord needs men like you to step up and work in his name to the best of your abilities.

"As you know, there is a meditation cell that the novices are forbidden to enter. Few monks, sometimes only one in a generation, are given the privilege of praying in the cell. I've discussed you with Brother Dadour, and we've decided that you shall have access to the meditation cell, although your time will be limited until we know that you can..." Father Mesrop seemed to search for a word, "... survive in the cell."

"I thank you for this honor," I replied, "although I am not worthy of it."

"We are not always aware of our worth," Father Mesrop said and I lowered my eyes.

Father Mesrop rang a small brass hand bell sitting on his desk and Brother Dadour entered the room. "Would you please show Brother Sevak to the cell?"

Brother Dadour bowed low and took my arm, guiding me from the Abbot's presence into the long, narrow corridors of G'ndevank.

"A great honor has been bestowed upon you, for currently only one living monk has been permitted into the cell," Brother Dadour told me. "Father Mesrop was the last monk to be allowed to use the cell, and that was more than sixty years ago. I have never crossed the threshold into the room and all I know of it, all I shall pass on to you, is what I have learned from Father Mesrop."

Brother Dadour spoke in guarded tones, as if he feared the walls of G'ndevank would hear his secrets and scream them to the world outside.

"Father Mesrop tells me that a supernatural calm falls upon those who enter the cell, allowing their thoughts to bring them closer to Him in a way that he has never felt in any other place in the world. But, he also warns that the feeling of serenity can be dangerous, for it is a...how did he describe it...an enticing calmness, as much to be feared as revel in." Brother Dadour saw the expression on my face, "No. I don't understand what that means. I expect you will, soon."

Despite the prohibited nature of the cell, it held a central location in the monastery, located next to the chapel of Saint Stepan. It was barred from the monks by a series of three intricate locks, to which Brother Dadour held a key, Father Mesrop held a key, and another key was stored in a location somewhere in the monastery known only to Father Mesrop. Before coming to retrieve me from Father Mesrop's presence, Brother Dadour had acquired all three of the keys.

Solitude was nothing new for me, or any monk, really. In addition to our chores in the fields and our communal prayers, each of us spent several hours each day in solitude, contemplating His creation and our own minuscule place in the vastness of the universe. I expected this cell, called the *khaghagh*, to be no different than my own cell where I had contemplated the world since I chose my path in the chaotic months following the independence of Armenia from the Soviet oppressors.

Brother Dadour opened the door and motioned for me to enter. The *khaghagh* held a sleeping pallet, a wash basin, a Bible, and a *khachkar*, the floral cross of Armenia which differs from the Spartan crosses and elaborate crucifixes of other nations. In its appearance and sparseness, the *khaghagh* was much like any other cell in G'ndevank. Had I seen a picture of it, I couldn't have identified it as anything except a standard monastic cell. Perhaps the ceiling was a little lower, the construction showed signs of its age, which monastic lore claimed predated the rest of the monastery by more than four centuries.

"Thank you, brother." I said to Brother Dadour as I crossed the threshold. As I did, a calm unlike any I had ever experienced settled over me.

"God be with you, Brother Sevak. I shall return for you shortly before dinner."

The wooden door closed without a sound and I knelt in front of the *khachkar*.

"*Eemasdootyoon Hor Hisoos*," I began the prayer for Wisdom, hoping to understand the great honor Father Mesrop had bestowed upon me. Whether or not I received an answer was irrelevant, for I felt comforted simply kneeling and saying the prayer.

My reverie was interrupted by a slight tapping on the door. I moved to open the door and found Brother Dadour on the other side.

"Will you join us for dinner, brother?"

"It has only been a few minutes, no more than half an hour."

"You are mistaken. Several hours have past since I left you. I have been knocking for at least five minutes. Please, join us for dinner."

I left the *khaghagh* with the strong sense that I had missed something, but a serenity imparted by the room seemed to remain with me even as I entered the monastery's refectory.

The entire population of the monks clustered at three long tables in a room designed to hold five times our number. Although we were not a silent order, there was little talking at meals, the sound of flatware and clay plates punctuated by the occasional voice asking for the bread to be passed. Nevertheless, after the hours I had spend in *khaghagh*, the clamor of the meal was deafening and it took all my resolve not to flee the room. By the time I finished eating, I had adjusted to the normal monastic sounds.

The next day, I again retreated to the *khaghagh* following lunch.

At one time, the room had windows to the outside, but over the course of centuries, they had been bricked and plastered over. No amount of touch up work, however, could make the room appear to be the same style as the rest of the monastery, even as the architecture of G'ndevank reflected different styles, they fit together in a way that the *khaghagh* did not. The room had an ancientness to it. Elsewhere, the weight of all those years might have been oppressive, but in the *khaghagh*, it somehow added to the sense of peacefulness, an almost oneness with the universe.

I began spending as much of my time as Brother Dadour would allow in the *khaghagh*. Both he and Father Mesrop warned me that the tranquility could prove addictive, and I understood their concerns when I was not in the retreat. When I was inside the retreat, I didn't care, for time, apprehension, doubt, all disappeared.

I didn't abandon my monastic duties, but they began to be less important to me than the serenity which I felt when I prayed to Him in the *khaghagh*. I could lose myself in contemplation, only to be brought back to the earthly world when Brother Dadour began knocking, sometimes pounding, on the door. The *khaghagh* was, in every conceivable way, my sanctuary.

During the Holy Season culminating in Easter, I spent less time than I would have liked in contemplation in the *khaghagh*. My monastic and religious duties required me to be with my fellow monks. When I was among them, I found myself battling a surliness I had never felt before, an unsociability that I never felt when I was in the *khaghagh*. I confessed to Father Mesrop, who gave me penance and a caution. "There is much good to gain from the *khaghagh* and I know you are strong enough, but you must not lose yourself." I did my penance and I focused on his words, but by July, I was again praying as often as I could in the *khaghagh*.

As I prayed, the true form of the *khaghagh* revealed itself to me. Wooden walls beneath the stone and plaster. There was a hole in the roof to let in the warmth and light of the sun and fresh air. In the center of the dirt floor was an ancient well that I somehow knew had gone bad and been sealed up a millennium ago, shortly after the consecration of St. Stepan's by Princess Sofia.

Rather than being alarmed by the change in the *khaghagh*'s aspect, I was comforted in a warm, womblike protection. For twenty years, I had lived in the monastery at Gndevaz, but for the first time, I realized it really was my home. It wasn't a question of being part of the community of monastic brethren, but rather being accepted by the holiness of the edifice itself. The prayers in the chapel, the toil in the fields, the monastic rule, they were all a part of the monastery, but they weren't the monastery itself.

I have heard that extended periods of solitude can cause a person to have visions and hear voices, but I do not think I imagined the gentle, feminine voice that spoke to me in an archaic Armenian, so old that it made the Church liturgy seem like the latest slang spoken on the streets of Yerevan.

I had thought that the peaceful atmosphere of the *khaghagh* came from the Lord of Peace, for the monastery has done His work for a millennium and Armenia has been in His hands for twenty centuries, but the *khaghagh* was holy long before the Blessed Thaddeus and the Blessed Bartholemew brought the Good News to the Armenians.

The voice told me of the legends of Astghig, wife of Vahagn, early Armenian heroes who were viewed as gods by the Armenians before the Word was brought to them. While Vahagn was a great warrior who slew dragons, Astghig was the source of life, the bringer of water, the civilizing influence on a race of hunters and warriors. I heard of her love for Vahagn and how she rushed to his aid in his fight against evil, shedding blood as she raced barefoot through the roses. How she sprinkled rose water over the land to bring love and harmony throughout Armenia. The voice spoke of how Astghig brings the morning dew and mist to create a peaceful, calm beginning for each day.

The well in the *khaghagh* was dedicated to Astghig and her spirit remains in its waters, even as they lay stagnant through the millennia, the unmoving waters reflective of the stillness of the room above them. Far from the *khaghagh* being dedicated to Christ's love, it remained under Astghig's protection, a sanctuary beyond strife.

By its very nature, though, this holy place, dedicated to the ancient Armenian Goddess of Peace, was united with His mission on Earth. To bring peace, love, and understanding to His creations.

In the two thousand years since Christianity had come to Armenia, it had stamped out nearly all traces of the pagan beliefs that predated it. Aside from the *khaghagh*, which few outside G'ndevank were aware of, only the ancient temple of Garni still existed.

Brother Dadour's knock roused me from my vision and I found myself once again in the familiar *khaghagh*. I opened the door.

"Please come with me," was all he said. A sense of sadness hung heavily over him and I wanted to close the door and retreat into the solitude of the *khaghagh*. Instead, we walked through the halls of the monastery. I saw monks at work in the fields, their bodies dripping with water, and watched as Brother Onik upended a bucket over Brother Patvakan.

"It is Vardavar?" I asked Brother Dadour. I realized I had lost all sense of time's passage.

"Yes, today is the Transfiguration of the Christ." He hurried on. I knew that Vardavar was more than the Christian holiday we celebrated. It was the holiday in honor of Astghig, who would sprinkle the world with water, bringing roses to life and peace to those who were thus baptized.

We arrived at the door to Father Mesrop's office and Brother Dadour paused. "Today should be a joyful day, and it still is for most of the monastery."

When he opened the door, I saw Father Mesrop slumped over his desk. There was no thought that he might be merely sleeping. Brother Dadour's demeanor and those of the other three monks in the room laid that possibility to rest.

I rushed to Father Mesrop's side and took his cold, flaccid, hand and began to recite the prayers for the dead.

"Brother Hovhan found him." Brother Dadour indicated one of the other monks in the room. "And now we must tell the rest of the brothers."

We left the Abbott's office and moved to the chapel of St. Stepan, with Brother Dadour asking Brother Zavur to ring the bell to summon the monks from the fields. The extant and mountainous nature of G'ndevank's property meant that it took close to half an hour for all the monks to filter into the church, some of them still drenched from the celebration of Vardavar or holding roses. Despite the nature of the holy day, the mood inside the chapel was somber as the monks waited for Brother Dadour to address them.

Father Mesrop's death was not entirely unexpected. Although none of us knew exactly when he was born, he had served as the head of the monastery since the 1930s, more than eighty years. Brother Dadour and I had once estimated his age as 105, but that was as much an article of faith as it was a mathematical certainty. He had been as much as part of the monastery as the cross hanging behind the altar or the *khaghagh*. More a part of the monastery than the *khaghagh*, for he was seen and known by all the brethren, not just the few.

Brother Dadour's announcement was greeted with a great wailing and cries of prayer. Pandemonium's gates had broken loose in the chapel, and yet I felt the calm I so associated with the *khaghagh* even as I was in the midst of the maelstrom.

Brother Dadour whispered to me, "Father Mesrop has left note of his desire for you to succeed him." I felt a piece of paper being pressed into my hand.

Father Mesrop's scrawling handwriting should have been difficult to read, but it wasn't. *"And if anyone is there who shares in peace, your peace will rest on that person; but if not it will return to you." The khaghagh has seen that you promote peace and your serenity will fill this House. "For everything there is a season and for every matter under Heaven." You have the strength within you to know what needs to be done and when, and when things need not be done. I have faith that you will protect this house.*

I walked out of the chapel and made my way down the hall. I passed the *khaghagh*, its closed door separating Astghig's peace from the chaos reigning in the monastery in the wake of Brother Dadour's proclamation. Father Mesrop's profession of faith rang in my head as I walked past the *khaghagh*'s door and made my way to my own cell to pray for the guidance I would needto lead the community with the serenity I learned from Astghig's calming waters and to keep the dangers of the world at bay, outside G'ndevank's ancient walls.

# — FOREST FOR THE TREES —
## Steven S. Long

*Every forest has its guardian, and often those guardians extend their protections to humans who treat the forest with respect and care. In Roman mythology, Silvanus is the guardian of the woods and fields. Silvanus protects the woods, but he also protects the fields and orchards that bounded the woods that the cattle that grazed nearby. Anyone who dealt kindly with the forest could count on Silvanus to protect his or her crops and kine.*

*In Germany, the forest is protected by the Waldgiest spirit. Like Silvanus, the Waldgeist has a reciprocal arrangement with travelers in their woods. The Waldgeist protects those who enter the forest with a pure heart, and people hang carvings of the Waldgeist over their doorways to obtain protection for their homes.*

*Meilikki is the Goddess of the Hunt in Finland. Like Silvanus, she extends her protection to cattle and to hunters and gatherers. Meilikki is a healing goddess who heals animals and people alike. In Hinduism, Aranyani can be heard walking through the forest because she wears tinkling bells on her ankles. She feeds people and animals and is described in the Rig Veda as always wandering but never lonely.*

*Some places have guardians that chase everyone away and that guard their locales with single-minded ferocity. But other places, like the forests of Finland, Rome, and India, reflect a gentler relationship. The forest can be a place of menace, but it can also be a source of sustenance and shelter, especially if tended properly through the centuries.*

T oday's the day. The thought made Dylan smile for the first time in... months? Years? He wasn't sure how long. Now that Cutler had finished and filed the final changes to his will he didn't have a good reason to wait any more.

He yawned and stretched as luxuriously as nausea and pain allowed. He didn't normally sleep in so late, but today of all days, why not? It wasn't as if he had anywhere to go.

He got up, moving slowly and carefully, the way he had to these days, and put on his clothes. Then he made his way into the bathroom to comb his hair and brush his teeth. He didn't really need to—he'd look pretty disgusting by the time someone found him regardless— but somehow it offended him not to.

After he finished his morning routine he opened the medicine cabinet and took out an amber plastic vial. Unlike the dozen other pill bottles in the cabinet, this one had no label. He twisted the cap off and dumped the contents into his left palm. He laid the pills out on the counter, one by one, in a straight line, evenly spaced.

Twenty-four pills, each carefully bought at the price of six hours of agony. Once the cancer had become so advanced that he didn't have any hope despite what the doctors kept telling him, he'd held back one painkiller here and there whenever he could tolerate it. He had no intention of withering away in slow torment like the people he saw at the clinic every week. His time was up, for all intents and purposes, so he might as well check out and see what awaited him on the other side.

He didn't know the best way to take them, though. Just swallow all of them with a cup of water? Grind them up and mix them with some food? The thought of eating made his nausea worse, so all at once it was.

As he reached for the blue plastic cup he glanced out the window and saw the woods half a block away. The early spring leaves had come out. He left the cup on its holder and went over to the window for a better look.

The woods. He'd had some sort of dream about them last night, but he couldn't remember it. In the usual way of dreams, it lingered in his mind as a vague memory, growing ever more vague as the day went on. He used to struggle to remember his dreams, even keeping a notebook and pen by the bed so he could write them down when he woke up. These days he didn't care.

He hadn't gone down to the woods in a long time—not since that kerfluffle with the Homeowners Association Board several years ago. But now, of all days, he felt the old call again, the one that had enticed him under the trees to play nearly every day when he was a kid.

He looked back at the pills on the counter and shrugged. He could take them this afternoon. Why not indulge his fantasies now?

Even in his current condition it didn't take long to walk to the edge of the woods. Clambering down the hillside through the trees to the forest floor was a little trickier; the last thing he wanted was to fall and break a leg. He stopped several times along the way to lean against a tree, catch his breath, let the pain die down. The hill hadn't seemed nearly so steep when he was ten.

At last he made it to the level ground near the creek, where the trees thinned out some. He stood there for a minute, just looking around, hearing the water rippling over the rocks, invigorated by the forest smell of loam and leaves. A flood of childhood memories accompanied the sensations: playing with his friends; fishing for minnows; watching birds and squirrels; bringing home feathers, odd-shaped stones, and other treasures only a boy could love. He used to keep them in a cigar box Dad had given him and look through them on rainy days sometimes. He'd thrown the whole collection out decades ago, too stupid as a twenty-something to recognize its value.

Barb Phillips and the rest of the people on the Board were idiots! Selling this plot of land to a developer would have been a tragedy. He didn't regret one penny of the money he'd spent to outbid that guy, though the stack of Past Due bills on the kitchen table back home argued that he'd made a bad decision. But what was done was done. Now that the Nature Preservation Trust owned this little patch of woods, no one would ever replace it with houses and lawns.

As he looked at the creek he realized it was... wrong. Something was off about it somehow. He stared at it for a few minutes, and walked up and down one section of the bank, until it hit him: the meanders through the forest had changed shape over time, obeying the immutable laws of erosion and water flow. God I'm old. I've lived here so long I can measure my life by geological processes.

"Hi," said a young voice behind him.

He turned around, slightly embarrassed that someone had found him wandering in the woods. Ten feet away stood a little girl in a green dress. Eight years old, maybe seven—or ten? He'd never spent much time around kids.

"Hi," he responded neutrally, looking all around. "Where's your mother?" he asked, all too aware of the presumptions people made these days about men found in the presence of small children.

"She's around," the girl said, stooping down to look at a bug. "She's always around."

"Maybe we should go find her. You don't want to get lost."

"I could never get lost here," she said. "What's your name?"

"Dylan," he said, smiling just a bit in spite of himself. "What's yours?"

"Sylvie."

"Well, it's very nice to meet you, Sylvie. That's a pretty name."

"Why are you down here? No one ever comes here but me."

"Just… reliving memories, I guess. I used to play in these woods every day when I was your age."

"For real?" she said, skepticism that he'd ever been that young plain on her face. Part of him shared the sentiment.

"It's true! I know a place where there's a pirate ship, a castle, a race car, and a space cruiser."

"No way!" she said, looking all around for them.

"Want me to show you?"

"Yeah!"

"Come on, it's this way," he said, gesturing east down the flow of the creek. It wasn't as easy a walk as it used to be; he had to make a few awkward hops from bank to bank or bank to rocky shoal to avoid patches of poison ivy or fallen branches. Sylvie practically skipped along, skirting the obstacles almost as if they didn't exist.

They rounded a bend in the creek and came to one of the long, straight parts of the stream. "See? There they are."

"Where?"

"Right there," he said, pointing.

"That's a log," Sylvie said, leaving the you silly grown-up part of the sentence unspoken.

"Don't look at it that way—look with your imagination," he said, squatting down so he could talk to her more easily. "Close your eyes and dream. It's not just a big log that crosses the creek like a bridge. It's the deck of good Captain… Morgan's pirate ship. He's going to fight the wicked Captain Crook. Draw your cutlass and prepare for battle!" Sylvie leaped into action, drawing a pretend sword. "En garde!" she said, giggling.

"Or maybe it's a castle. From the tallest tower the Princess Sylvie looks out at a fearsome army of trolls preparing to attack. You have to defend your people and save the kingdom!" Grinning, Sylvie shifted stance and mimicked drawing a bow and aiming.

"Sssss—thunk! You got one of the biggest trolls with that shot!"

'Yay!" she said, dancing around.

"See what I mean? With your imagination and that log, you can go anywhere and do anything."

"Yeah!" she said, running over to the log. She had a little trouble getting to the top—it was still a huge log, despite the passage of decades—but once she did her imagination took over. Dylan looked on as she pretended to drive it, ran back and forth along it while monsters chased her, or simply sat and watched the creek flow underneath it. It shocked him to realize he hadn't thought about himself or the disease for at least ten minutes.

But even the biggest fallen log in the forest couldn't hold a child's attention forever. "What else is there around here?" she asked, jumping down onto the creek bank. Dylan winced a little, thinking how that kind of stunt would hurt his ankles these days.

"Want to know where to find the best mud for making mud pies in the whole forest?" he said.

"Yes!"

They continued east down the creek. In a few places branches and silt had clogged up the stream, slowing the water and creating deep pools. Maybe I should bring my rake down here and clear some of that gunk out.

"See here?" he said when they reached the spot he remembered. "That part of the bank is perfect: soft mud, and no tree roots in the way. Anytime you want some mud, this is the place to get it."

"Okay!" Sylvie said.

"Hey, check this out," Dylan said, crouching down for a closer look. "Do you know what kind of animal made these tracks?"

"Uh-uh," she said, shaking her head. "Squirrel?"

"No, squirrels' feet aren't that big, and they don't weigh enough to leave such deep marks. They're raccoon tracks. You know what a raccoon is?"

Sylvie nodded.

"People think they come down to creeks like this to wash their food, but really they're just foraging or playing. This raccoon was probably trying to catch himself a crayfish for dinner."

"Yuck!" Sylvie said, making a face.

"Well, raccoons like 'em," Dylan said with a grin. As he watched her play by the creek a little piece of her sense of wonder settled into his soul, bringing with it a tranquility he hadn't felt in years. This is far, far too fine a place to leave behind, he thought, then realized to his chagrin that he'd stolen from Dickens.

"This is for you," Sylvie said, holding out a water-smoothed stone. She'd carefully washed it in the creek, then dried it on her dress. He took it in his hands. Green, smooth, cool to the touch, it looked and felt nothing like any of the dozens of stones he'd found down here as a boy. "Thank you," he said softly. "I'll treasure it."

A flash of red caught their eyes. A cardinal with some strands of grass in its beak flew past them and landed in a nearby tree. "Look, he's building a nest!" Sylvie said.

"He sure is. That means there'll be some baby birds soon."

"I can't wait to see them!"

"Neither can I," Dylan said, surprised to discover that he meant it. He stood there for a moment, thinking about those birds… and the fruit on the blackberry patches later in the season… and the glorious tapestry of colors in autumn. It's things like the woods that make life worth living despite the pain.

Like a demon summoned by his thoughts, the pain chose that moment to stab him in the gut. He hadn't taken any painkillers since late yesterday.

"Are you okay, Dylan?" Sylvie said.

"I'm fine, sweetie, but I need to get home. Can I take you back to your mother?"

"No, I'm gonna stay and play some more. Will you be here tomorrow?"

"I will," he said with a smile. "We can look for turtles. Would you like that?"

"Yes!" she said, jumping up and down and then giving him a hug.

"See you tomorrow, then. Be careful down here, okay?"

"I will."

Dylan climbed back up the hill, sometimes holding onto trees to get past the steepest places. At the top, before he left the forest and walked up the street to his house, he turned and looked back at Sylvie. He waved, and she waved back. He smiled and headed home.

When Dylan had gone, Sylvie walked over to a huge old beech tree, one whose roots reached many feet from its thick trunk. She put her hand on the silvery-grey bark—and slowly faded away, like a dream upon waking.

The leaves of the beech tree rustled as if in the wind, speaking a language no human had ever understood or ever would. This man has given of himself to save us. Now we will save him, and the circle be maintained.

Throughout the woods, all the other trees rustled their agreement.

# — IRON FELIKS —
## Anatoly Belilovsky

One of the most controversial statues in Russia is known as Iron Feliks. The statue was built in 1958 by Yvgeny Vuchetich. It's a statue of a man who was responsible for the deaths of thousands of people—Felix Dzerzhinsky, the head of the first Soviet secret police organization (it was succeeded by the KGB).

Felix Dzerzhinsky was born in 1877 in what is now Belarus. He devoted his life entirely to Marxist revolution, spending years in brutal prisons and in exile in Siberia because of his revolutionary activities. After the October Revolution of 1917, the Bolsheviks, led by Lenin, formed the All-Russia Extraordinary Commission to Combat Counter-revolution and Sabotage, better known as Cheka. Cheka's mission was to eliminate counter-revolutionary elements, and Dzerzhinsky was put in charge.

During the Russian Civil War that followed the October Revolution, Cheka, which earned the nickname "The Red Terror", tortured and executed thousands of prisoners without trial. The estimated number of people murdered ranges from thousands to hundreds of thousands. Dzerzhinsky and Lenin were unrepentant about the methods of Cheka, claiming that they would eliminate any opposition by any means necessary. "We represent in ourselves organized terror," said Dzerzhinsky.

Dzerzhinsky was nicknamed "Iron Feliks", and the statue made in his honor was an iron giant, weighing fifteen tons. The statue was toppled in August 1991, during the massive protests that followed an attempted coup against Mikhail Gorbachev. The statue, along with other fallen monuments, ended up at Muzeon Park.

Since 1991, there have been many attempts to restore the statute to the park, most recently in 2013. To date, lawmakers have rejected all proposals, fearing that the statue will attract protests. Dzerzhinsky never saw himself as a villain. He saw himself as the guardian of a beleaguered state. Today he is hated, feared, and, by some people, loved.

The old man looked both ways before crossing Politekhnichesky Street. His dog waited, the leash slack between the collar and the old man's hand. When the old man stepped off the curb, the dog followed.

A flock of pigeons worried at a heel of bread in the middle of the street, and as the old man and the dog walked past them toward Lubyanka, and as the birds fluttered into the air, a little girl peered out from behind one of the spruces. She followed the pigeons' flight until they disappeared behind the trees, then turned toward the dog.

"Babushka, look!" she exclaimed. "Sobachka!"

She jumped in place, looking from the dog to the old man and back again.

The old man looked as if he had been carved all in straight lines and acute angles, and as the pair approached she danced aside as if to keep from cutting herself against the edges of his shadow-colored silhouette.

An elderly woman emerged from the shade of the spruce.

"Some sobachka this is," the old woman said to the girl. "Everything is diminutive for you now, isn't it?" She reached for the girl, pulled her into a protective embrace. "A sobaka will bite your face off," she said, "but a sobachka will just lick it." She turned to the old man. "This sobachka looks like he's done his share of biting."

"Not when he is with me," the old man said, and to the old woman's ear it sounded as if it came from deeper places than most.

The old woman's eyes turned to the dog. The dog returned her gaze.

The old woman looked away first.

"Good thing that leash is strong, for a dog with eyes like this," she said and looked down at the little girl, relaxing her hold.

The little girl slipped free and took a step forward.

"What breed is it? I've never seen its like," the old woman added.

"Georgian Mountain dog," the old man said.

"Don't trust Georgians," the old woman said. "Though I suppose dogs are different. Nothing but savages in those hills. You sure the dog is safe?"

The old man lifted his hand. The leash wound three times around it.

The old woman turned to look behind her, at the black bulk of Feliks Edmundovich Dzerzhinsky's statue that stood watch over Lubyanka square. The sun shone upon it, as always in Moscow between Lenin's Birthday in April and Victory Day in May, summer-bright and winter-cold. It brought a blue glow to spruces whose branches had spent the winter peering greenish-gray from under mounds of snow, and dabbed the roundabout under the monument in decadent pointillistic swirls of pansies. Behind the statue, the beige facade of the FSB Headquarters (but no one ever got used to calling it that, and still referred to it as the KGB more often than not,) turned a delicate shade of peach.

"I don't suppose you'd consider walking with us toward Iron Feliks?" the old woman said. "My granddaughter wanted to go play in the pansies at its feet. I am afraid of the cars in the square, they drive like the possessed here, but maybe for the four of us they'd slow down?"

"Yes, yes please," the little girl said. She pirouetted toward the old woman. "Can we go to Iron Feliks?" She turned her head toward the old man. "Please?"

The old man looked at the dog, then nodded. "We can do that," he said. "Did your grandmother teach you how to cross the street correctly?"

"Yes," the little girl said. "You look both ways," she said and turned left and right with slow exaggerated bows. "And you keep your feet on the 'zebra' and you hold on to an adult at all times." She patted the dog. "He's an adult, right?"

The old man nodded again, his wrinkled face creasing into a half-smile.

"So I'll hold on to him," said the little girl. She stepped forward and took hold of the dog's collar. "Why do they call Dzerzhinsky the Iron Feliks?" she asked. "Babushka says that's because he's a statue, but then she crosses herself every time we pass him, and he isn't even a saint…"

The old woman crossed herself again. "How do you explain such things to a child?" she said. "She's never even been to a funeral, the lucky girl, and on a good day can maybe count to a hundred. How do you tell her what 'Revolutionary Terror' means when she's not afraid of a dog with fangs the size of my pinkie? 'Fiery Felix,' 'Sword of the Revolution.' Rivers of blood in basements." She glanced at the statue again, sighed, raised her arm and brought it down again dismissively. "All she knows is skazki," she added. "Everything starts with 'Once upon a time, in a kingdom far away…' and ends with 'To the wedding I went, mead and beer I drank, down my mustache it flowed and none in my mouth.' Nothing but fairy tales." She ran her hand across her lips as if wiping an imaginary mustache, smiled, and sighed.

The dog's head rose. He turned to look at the old man. The old man cupped his chin, turned to the little girl. The little girl raised her eyebrows; her eyes went wide, twin circles of blue.

"Perhaps," the old man said, "a fairy tale is what we should tell her?"

"Yes yes please," the little girl said, her hands reaching, one to the old man, one to her grandmother. "Please tell me a skazka. Please please!"

The old woman turned and started toward Lubyanka. "Why not? She can listen on the way," she said. "As Pushkin wrote, 'A skazka is a lie—'"

"'—but in it is a hint, and a lesson,'" the little girl quoted. "But mostly I hope it's interesting. And maybe a little scary."

The old woman sighed. "Interesting and scary," she said. "Yes, that's Iron Feliks all right."

The little girl ran to catch up with the old woman, took her hand. The old man and the dog took longer steps until they drew abreast with them. Under the little girl's questioning stare they walked another few steps in silence.

The little girl drew a breath to speak, opened her mouth. The old man spoke first.

"Once upon a time..." he said and paused a moment, looking at the old woman "...there was great wickedness in the land—" he continued.

"That's what Grandma says," the little girl interrupted. "Except she says there's great wickedness in the land now."

The old woman's shoulders convulsed again.

"Be as it may," the old man said. "Now, do you want to hear the story or not?"

The little girl nodded.

"There was," he repeated, "great wickedness. And the people said that the wickedness comes from some people thinking they are better than others..."

"But some people are better than others," the little girl said. "Everybody says so."

"Yes," the old man said. "And that, they said, is at the root of wickedness, and everyone must be equal and then everyone would be good. And for that, you need a Revolution."

"Lenin made the Revolution, right?" the little girl asked.

"With a little help," the old man said. "And Lenin's friends could only be people with fiery hearts, cool heads, and clean hands."

The little girl looked at her hands. "Babushka always makes me wash my hands," she announced. "Especially before I sit down to eat."

"That means your grandmother cares about you," the old man said. "So Lenin decided he'd keep his hands clean, and he built Iron Feliks: At his front a hammer to beat down heads that stick up, and a sickle to cut off ones that won't bend; at his heart a steam engine like a parovoz, and the rest of him is cast iron: feed him coal, let him drink water, and he'll go all day and all night, with a fire in his heart."

They reached another curb and stopped. The four looked left and right, their turns almost comically simultaneous. The old woman tightened her grip on the little girl's hand before they went into the square.

"What about the cool head?" the little girl said. "Who got that?"

"That was Stalin," the old man said.

The old woman nodded, sighed, and crossed herself again. "Oh yes," she said. "Cold. He was the one who drove Iron Feliks, used some people as cogs, some people as rails, some people as fuel." She looked up, her eyes distant. "You'd give anything to be a cog," she added quietly.

The dog stepped forward onto the flower bed.

"Look, we are here!" the little girl exclaimed. "Look at all these pansies!" She bent down. "Babushka, I'm going to make you a buketik," she said. "I'll only pull up the nicest pansies. All kinds: red, purple, white. Just for you."

"See what I mean?" the old woman said. "At this age, it's all diminutives. Buketik, not bouquet. Ah, to be young again."

The little girl drew herself up to her full height to look up at her grandmother. She put her hands on her hips.

"But, babushka," she said, drawing out her words, "these are pansies. They are tiny tsvetochki; you can make a big bouquet from big tsveti like roses or peonies, but from little pansies you can only make a little buketik."

"And an answer for everything," the old woman said. "Children," she said, and gave another bark of mirthless laughter.

"But do you know," the old man said, "when to stop pulling up pansies?" The old woman and the dog both looked up at his voice, but the girl squatted and reached down.

"Well," she said, "I have to make a buketik for Babushka, and for mommy and for daddy and one for Grandpa's grave—he died in the War—"

"And soon there won't be any pansies around Iron Feliks, and won't he be cross then?" the old man said.

"You can't make buketiki without pulling up tsvetochki," the little girl said. She chose a purple flower to add to the red and yellow flowers already in her hand. "But do go on," she said. "What happened to Iron Feliks?"

"He pulled up too many flowers," he said.

The old woman's head whipped around to face him. Her hand flew to her open mouth.

The little girl looked up. "How's that?" she said.

"He was supposed to pull up weeds, but he pulled too many flowers instead," the old man said. "Soon, there was no one to do the work."

"Well, I can understand him," the little girl said with an inflection clearly copied from an adult, and reached down again. "Weeds are so much harder to pull, and they are useless. Can't make a buketik out of weeds, right?"

"No," said the old man. "No, you cannot."

"But did they punish Iron Feliks?" the little girl asked. "What did they do to him? When I misbehave, my mother puts me in a corner..." She trailed off, her mouth quirking downward.

"They didn't do anything," the old man said. "Just let him rust."

"And what about the others?" the little girl said. "What are their names?"

"Lenin died and went into the Mausoleum," the old man said. "He is under glass, his hands will never get dirty. And Stalin..." He hesitated.

The dog looked at him.

"Please please," she said. "Tell me about Stalin! Did he gather flowers, too?"

The dog's tail stopped wagging.

The old man sighed. "I think I'll let your grandmother tell the story," he said and clutched the dog's leash.

The little girl straightened. "Here, take these!" she said and handed her grandmother a bouquet of pansies. "Can you tell me about Stalin?" she continued. "Did he make proper bouquets?"

The old woman chuckled. "Proper bouquets? That's one way of putting it," she said. Her hand went to her temple. "Must be this sun," she said. "I'm getting a headache. Let's go back."

"Oh, babushka," the little girl said. "Please? Just one more buketik..."

"You should listen to your grandmother," the old man said.

They started back across the square.

There were pigeons in the street again. They batted a rotten biscuit in zigzags back and forth along the asphalt, racing for crumbs and fighting for precedence, and for a moment their coos and wingbeats remained the loudest sound that could be heard.

In mid-crossing, the dog stopped short, his ears pricking up. An instant later, pigeons stopped pecking. The old man stopped as well. The old woman pulled the little girl toward her.

The squeal of tires came first, from the corner of Novaya Ploschad', and then a sleek white sports car (a serpent ondoyant vert vorant a child gules) sped into the square, a swarm of bits of paper and cigarette butts roiling in its wake. Bass notes of a nightclub-favorite song beat themselves against the car's closed windows, toned too dark to see the driver, their echo adding to the flutter of startled pigeons' wings. The car careened straight at the little girl and her grandmother; the old woman's mouth opened in a silent O as she reached forward with her free hand as if to ward it off.

The dog stepped forward. The fur rose on its neck, it growled, far too softly to hear inside the car, but in an instant the car swerved, tires screaming, slewed into the flower bed, fishtailed in a spray of soil and petals, scraped a shower of sparks off the pavement as it leaped off the curb, and sped away to disappear on the other side of the statue.

The dog shook himself and looked up at the man again. The old man brushed his free hand down each lapel, once, and adjusted his hat.

The old woman took a breath, then let it out slowly. Her hand drew into a fist; she shook at the dying roar of the retreating car.

"A curse on you!" she said, her voice shaking in anger. "A curse on all you bull-necked New Russians, on all the merchants who make you pay whatever they want for food and clothes! On all you mafiozniki, on all the hooligans who stop good people in the street, on all the bribe-takers and look-the-other-ways, let the devil take you, devil and Stalin!" She paused, looked down, her forehead creasing, eyes squeezing shut. "Things might be better if he'd come back," she said quietly. She let go of her granddaughter's hand, grasped and kneaded the little girl's shoulders. "Lots of people wish he'd come back," she whispered.

There was a silence for a second or two, deeper, it seemed, than any silence could be on a Moscow street. A cloud slipped across the sun; shadows grew indistinct, the statue darkened, and the facade behind it lost its peach hue, turning exactly the color of a sliver of bone protruding from a compound fracture.

"Babushka! Babushka! Look," the little girl yelled. "The nice sobachka is smiling!"

# — THE CROOKED SMILE KILLERS —
## James Lowder

*The face of crime always horrified Tristram Holt, known to Chicago's underworld as the Corpse, but never more so than when small-time hoods and sharpsters began mutating into monsters. Can the Scourge of Evil track down the criminal mastermind behind their transformations before the city is remade into a realm of living nightmares?*

## — 1 —
### Slaves of the Silver Key

The blonde leveled the still-smoking revolver at the man sprawled at her feet. "Of course I love you," she said.

Everything about Julia Halloran seemed to proclaim those words a lie. Her voice was cold and even, her piercing blue-gray eyes unmisted by tears. Her hand stayed steady as she trained the .38 at what remained of the dying man's head. The first shot had been a little high. A small chunk of his skull was gone, but his features were intact. She took careful aim, intent on correcting that mistake.

Julia paused then, her mask of resolve slipping just enough to reveal her pain. She choked back a sob and searched her husband's eyes one last time for some hint of understanding. She could finish it without going mad if Sean recognized that she really was acting out of love.

Julia didn't find what she was looking for in his eyes. Head haloed by a spreading crimson pool, Sean Halloran stared up at the apartment's water-stained ceiling. His expression betrayed no misery, no surprise, only a profound weariness. Slowly his gaze moved to his wife. Her love had been the lifeblood of his dreams, at least the ones he'd not bartered away or allowed to wither. Now those last surviving hopes abandoned him.

With their passing, Sean Halloran's eyes became fixed, as inexpressive as stone.

Not so his mouth, which was already quirked up at one end in an exaggerated, unnatural smirk. That smirk grew. It pushed up into his cheek, lips stretching until they fissured at a dozen bloodless faults. His jaw shifted as the gash of his mouth crept higher. The sound of bones cracking drowned out his bubbling, labored breaths.

The sight robbed Julia of her resolve. Her arms dropped to her sides, the gun dangling from numb fingers. "God help us," she whispered. "Too late."

"Yes, Julia Halloran," said a sepulchral voice. "He belongs to Hell now."

A figure wrapped in a ragged black cloak slipped through the open window leading to the fire escape. He adjusted the aim of his twin pistols as he emerged from the darkness and crossed the room, one gun fixed on the dying man, the other on the would-be murderer. His movements were effortless and menacing, a drop of poison gliding along a dagger's edge.

For an instant Julia mistook the weird figure for Death itself. The threadbare cloak fluttered behind him like wings as he approached. Beneath the brim of his black fedora, his gaunt face was cadaverous, with blue-white flesh pulled tight over jutting bones. An awful, inhuman light—a crimson promise of justice, swift and merciless—flickered in the voids of his eyes.

He loomed over Sean Halloran for a moment and studied the dying man's growing hideousness. The whites of Sean's eyes had darkened to the purple and yellow of old bruises. The darkness devoured the brown of his irises. It crept hungrily across his face and body, staining his skin. Wherever the purple discoloration appeared, the flesh spasmed. Sean's mouth shuddered, too. It had shifted so much that it ran in a nearly vertical line, from his chin to the side of his nose. The inhuman maw gabbled and chuckled in a language heard only in the nightmares of the hopelessly mad.

The cloaked stranger nodded slowly, as if he understood every word.

There was no hesitation as he squeezed the trigger. Three bullets obliterated Sean Halloran's head and silenced the eerie gibbering. The body trembled, tried to rise. Arms dark and bloated to near bursting struggled to push the torso from the floor. Finally, it collapsed and lay still.

All during the execution, the stranger kept his second automatic trained on the woman. The muzzle was poised a handbreadth from her face. "Your gun," he said without looking at her. "Drop it."

The .38 slipped from her fingers and thudded to the floor.

"The police will be here soon to investigate the gunshots," he said. "I need some information from you before they arrive."

"I know who you are now. I didn't at first, but now I know. You're that vigilante—the one the papers call the Corpse. The *Tribune* said you'd left town and you weren't coming back."

"They were wrong."

"Yes, Sean said so, too. He said you'd be back." She coughed a hollow, bitter laugh. "He was afraid of you."

"With good reason." Holstering his guns, the Corpse crouched to examine the body.

"Sean told me you killed Goose Vanderbilt."

"Vanderbilt was a criminal, a murderer, like Sean," he said as he studied the dead man's fingers. They were patterned with small blotches even darker than his skin's purple cast. "If you've done nothing wrong, you have nothing to fear from me."

"That's why you had to come back. We've all done something wrong. Everyone in Chicago." Julia looked down at her hand, still aching a little from the pistol's recoil. "A lot of it's as bad as the things that Sean and those friends of his had gotten into. Whatever rotten business it was that damned my poor, sad darling."

The crimefighter reached into Sean's shirt for the thin chain circling his neck. He knew the chain would be there and what he'd find attached to it: an elaborately wrought silver key. Unlike the others he'd seen, though, this one was spotted with black paste. He yanked it free. "Where did this come from?"

"The key? I don't know, but he's had it a few weeks." Julia moved dazedly to a cabinet and took a box down from a shelf. "I first noticed it the day he smashed this."

She removed the handkerchief that covered the lidless box like she was pulling back a winding sheet. Inside lay the ruins of a homemade crystal radio set, the coil wrapped around an empty Albers Flapjack Flour package. "Sean wanted to be an announcer. He built this so he could listen to the Cubs games through an earpiece and call them for me. The day he broke it they were playing the Robins at Wrigley." She set the box beside her husband's body. "He was never good enough to play, but he could have been a great announcer. It's all he ever really wanted. Any trouble he got himself into—before whatever that bastard Vanderbilt got him mixed up in—came from big ideas to get money for voice lessons or a suit for interviews. But then he just gave up. Smashed the radio and wouldn't talk about it again."

"The rest of it started then, too," the Corpse said. "The smile."

Julia nodded. The crooked smile was a constant after that, a badge Sean had shared with Vanderbilt and the other men who came to collect him for their late-night jobs. She'd come to loathe that expression, and to fear it. She hadn't been to church since leaving Ireland, but she recognized the touch of the Devil readily enough.

Out in the hallway the sound of small footfalls ended in pounding and a shout: "Ma," a child bleated, "let me in quick! The bulls are all over the street!"

A door creaked open to admit the boy. Before it slammed shut again, the noise from within the apartment grew momentarily louder. "Is everybody happy?" Ted Lewis asked from a scratched and skipping phonograph record. "Happy—happy—happy. . . ?"

The question cut through Julia's shock. She gazed at the dead body with suddenly clear eyes, then scanned the room. She was startled, as if she were seeing her squalid surroundings for the first time. "Sweet Jesus, but it's hot in here," she said. "And that awful smell."

The stench was the usual tenement funk and the less specific miasma of disease, decay, and death that lingered in such places. Though the Hallorans' room was cleaner than most in the building, the smell there was no less oppressive. It had long ago permeated the floorboards and plaster. The tenants could no more escape it than they could silence the persistent drone of drunken shouts and curses, the bawl of hungry children, the harsh liquid hack of the sick, and the sobs of desperation that thrummed through the pipes and bled from every crack and corner joint.

Wordlessly the Corpse watched the tears well in Julia's eyes and roll down her cheeks. The tears weren't so much the mark of her sadness flowing out as the despair flooding in. Whatever defenses she'd erected against the misery of her life were disintegrating.

The key cupped in the Corpse's gloved hand glowed with a sickly blue radiance. He'd seen this before with the keys he'd taken from Vanderbilt and three of Halloran's other associates. It was feeding off her sorrow somehow. He slipped the key into the pocket of his bullet-torn coat and withdrew a silver tube. He emptied its contents onto the dead body at the center of the room. There was thunder now in the hall, the heavy-footed charge of policemen in the stairwell.

Julia followed the Corpse over to the open window. "Find the monster that did this to him," she said.

He could see that she was already lost to whatever strangeness had sunk its claws into the city. "I promise you justice," he replied. That promise sounded very much like the threat it really was.

When the police broke down the door to the apartment, they found only the remains of Sean Halloran, upon which writhed a few dozen yellow-white maggots—the calling card of the Corpse. The vigilante and the widow were gone. The Corpse was, at that moment, dropping down into the alley from the bottom rung of the building's fire escape. He paused for only a moment before he stepped over Julia Halloran's body, a still, broken heap after her silent leap into oblivion. Then he turned his back on her shattered form and headed toward the low-rent theater district on South State, the locus of true magic in Chicago.

— 2 —

## HEARTS AND SPADES

The Mysterious Pharos sat crosslegged at the front edge of the stage, dead center, bathed in the harsh glare of a spotlight. He drew a playing card from the deck in his left hand, presented it to the empty seats arrayed before him, and asked, "This isn't your card either, is it?" After a moment, he flicked the card into the darkness, where it joined a scattering of rejects, then drew again from the steadily diminishing deck. He was too caught up in his odd little game to notice the figure standing to the rear of the stage, out of the light.

The Corpse was at home in the shadows. He'd escaped into their embrace more than two years earlier, when he was still just Tristram Holt, crusading assistant district attorney. He scarcely remembered his flight from the laboratory run by mobster "Schemer" Drucci. His memories of the lab, on the other hand, remained vivid. It was a chamber of horrors where a trio of doctors alternately pumped him full of chemicals and toyed with his nerves and sinews just to hear him scream. Only later did he learn that the butchers were trying to transform him into a living bomb intended to destroy the city's secret Crime Commission. The doctors experimented on Holt for days before he escaped, albeit momentarily. Drucci's soldiers gunned him down on the brink of safety. They thought him dead after his bullet-riddled body disappeared into the murk of the Chicago River. The chemical slurry running through Holt's veins and the toughness he'd built up in the trenches of the Great War kept him alive long enough to crawl from the stinking river into a hobo den in the Levee. There, in that notorious cesspit of vice, he created a new identity for himself, one in keeping with the dead man's pallor that clung to his flesh and the cold passion for justice that gripped his soul: the Corpse.

The dark had been the Corpse's ally in his war against the gangs and the stranger, more terrible things that plagued Chicago. So it was little surprise that the Mysterious Pharos had not noticed the Corpse creeping through the gloomy theater, past the tossed cards and up onto the stage. Someone else had, though. Someone equally at home in the dark as the vigilante.

"It's a downbeat show, I admit," said the woman as she stepped from of the wings. "But it's better than the alternative."

Samantha van Ayers wore a magician's assistant costume. It was more revealing than some, less gaudy than most, if you discounted the especially large black ostrich feather jutting from the gauze headband. She appeared comfortable enough in the get-up, but it still seemed wrong for her. She was a little too short, not quite leggy enough to carry off the role of statuesque stage dressing. A casual observer might have dismissed Samantha as hopelessly plain, until she flashed her eyes. They revealed a young woman possessed of an indomitable self-confidence born of hard travels and harder fights. It was the defiance they blazed, particularly when she smiled and cocked her head just a little, that did it. That simple shift of expression banished the illusion of plainness. It wasn't a feat of legerdemain or a clever illusion; no one mistook Samantha for anything but remarkable once they noticed her eyes.

She took in the Corpse with a particularly defiant look as she crossed the stage to him. "Sometimes when he gets in these moods, he takes out the rabbits and—well, you wouldn't want to be here for that. Or maybe it'd be a ghoulish enough spectacle that you'd enjoy it."

"Maybe. Did you decipher the symbols on the key?"

Samantha started to reply, but Pharos broke in, "Do I hear the voice of the dead? Is it the Scourge of Evil himself, here on my stage?" He got to his feet and quick-shuffled the partial deck in his hands. "I have something for you."

Pharos cut the deck, flipped up the top card, and announced, "This is no one's, sir, if not yours. The death card for the dead man." When his audience did not react, the magician turned the card over. It wasn't the one he had expected. "Damn it," he muttered.

"No, Fred, you called it correctly," said his assistant. "You just forgot that you sent it over here." Samantha held up the ace of spades in one satin-gloved hand. She seemed to produce the card from nowhere. "Nicely done."

"I need information on the keys, Sam," the Corpse said tersely. "They're linked to this plague of suicides. Worse things, too. The people driven to slitting their wrists are the lucky ones. The keys are transforming some of the yeggs and thugs carrying them into monsters, and the changes are accelerating. So tell me what you found out. I don't have time to stand around here while you humor your boss."

"I know you think I'm a washed-up clown," Pharos sneered. "Well, this washed-up clown discovered the keys' secret."

"He's right," Samantha said. The silver key she presented was a twin to the one the Corpse had taken from Sean Halloran. "If you look closely enough, you'll see a series of tiny engravings. Some of the symbols are ancient glyphs, but the others—Fred recognized them for what they are."

"Mathematical notation," the magician announced with theatrical bombast. "Parts of complicated formulae. There were also segments of what I conclude will be a tesseract when completed. If you have any other keys, I'd wager a week's worth of house receipts they carry different sections of some larger equation and other pieces of the geometric shape."

The Corpse handed Pharos the Halloran key. After studying it for a time, the magician said, "I'd need a magnifying glass to be certain, but the formulae and segments look a little different on this one, just as I said they would. I'll tally up the amount you owe me for our little wager, but this—" Pharos smirked and slowly, sensually, licked the key. "This gives me a good idea of how you can pay off the debt. I should have known you'd be the type to kick the gong around, dead man."

Samantha snatched the key away from the magician. She glanced at the blotched metal and returned it to the Corpse. "Opium?"

"Halloran's fingers had *yen shee* stains. Vanderbilt's, too. Kang Hai controls the opium dens around town. Perhaps this is his doing." The Corpse scowled. He'd battled the mastermind several times in the past year, often to a standstill.

"Some of the glyphs I saw on the key come from the East," Samantha noted.

"I've seen one of them before myself, when I was in Europe after the War. The Yellow Sign, I think it was called."

"The symbols come from several traditions. Some are totally new to me. They're a weird mix, arranged in patterns built up around the math."

"Which I deciphered," Pharos said.

"Got it," the crimefighter growled. "Now go back to playing with your cards."

The magician smirked. "This has to be killing you—admitting you needed me."

"No, but we're done with this goddamn game." The Corpse drew his pistols and pointed them at the Pharos. "One more word and I'll cut you in half. I promise, not even God will be able to put you back together after this trick."

Samantha guided her boss away from the vigilante and spoke quietly with him for a moment. She handed him a small bottle—dark glass, without a label. The magician clutched it to his chest as he hurried down from the stage and exited the theater through the doors that led to the adjacent oddity museum. The collection of pickled punks and medical mistakes would be empty this early in the evening; the cheap amusement parlors crammed together on South State were more popular with the late-night crowd. Pharos's magic act didn't even go on with its first show until ten. So there'd be no customers to raise an eyebrow as the magician shared his bottle with the trio of sideshow rejects who worked the museum and the theater for him.

The swinging door had scarcely creaked closed behind Pharos before Samantha held up a hand to the Corpse. "Don't even think about starting with me, Tris. I wouldn't have had to give him the bottle if you would have just let him take his bows for recognizing the symbols. It really was him, you know. He remembered them from some book he'd read about lost cities and crazy mathematics, of all things. I tracked down a copy."

She led the crimefighter into the wings and through a maze of props and crates. Whatever glamour the objects presented on stage was lost here. The base of a gaudily painted vanishing cabinet, a prototype labeled as the property of the Great Doppo, had been gnawed by something small and hungry. The arm chopper guillotine was spattered with the reminder of an illusion gone wrong. The partial faces of wickedly goateed magicians and leering crimson devils overlooked the jumble from torn posters on the back wall.

Their staring eyes followed the pair as they made their way to a table, upon which rested some papers and a single musty volume, *The Geometry of Nowhere* by R. E. Beckford.

"What do you know about the author?" the Corpse asked.

"American professor. Taught at Northwestern. Brilliant. Murdered in 1893. His severed head was found by British tourists outside the grounds of the World's Fair. I looked him up when I lifted the book from the Newberry." Samantha sorted through the papers until she came to an intricate, carefully rendered arrangement of lines and curves. There were symbols spaced along the design at regular intervals. "The mathematical rigmarole on the keys is only part of it. You plot out the code on them and you get this." She tapped the paper. "I don't understand it all yet, but there's some familiar stuff here. I've seen the underlying pattern on sacred objects woven by Chippewa shamans. They call them *bawaajige nagwaagan*. Dream snares."

"Of course. The keys steal the dreams of the small-time hoods, pushing them to destroy their lives. The opium would make those dreams stronger or maybe diminish the dreamer's resistance." The Corpse stuffed the drawing into his pocket. "It has to be Kang Hai's work."

"Well, there's a difference between conscious hopes and the unconscious, but in this case, the magic seems to be targeting them both. I don't know about it being Kang Hai, though. He might be familiar with the magic, but isn't he usually a lot more precise in selecting his marks? More businesslike?"

The Corpse shrugged. "Maybe we haven't figured out the whole scheme yet."

"This seems too wild to fit his M.O.," Samantha said. "I started to get a feeling that something was wrong not long after you left for that jaunt to the East Coast a couple months ago, and, like you said, it's getting worse. Whatever this enchantment is, it's starting to affect the entire city—the people susceptible to despair, anyway. I caught Fred out on stage earlier weeping like a lost child."

"He is a lost child. But you're not his mother."

"I owe him," Samantha said. "You do, too, and for more than just his help with the keys. There was that time with the Mushroom Men, for starters."

"A favor I returned by squaring him with Branch and Crump after he scammed them last Halloween. If not for me, they would have torn out his heart and fed it to their pals underneath the Resurrection Cemetery."

"He's a good man. A friend. You used to understand that."

"He's a drunk and a grifter. Wise up. You're wasting your gifts on him. You have the power to make this city a paradise and you piss it away conjuring whiskey and fixing botched card tricks for a hoary-eyed huckster."

"I'll bet the lunatic handing out the keys thinks he's creating a paradise, at least for himself. As for the hootch and the tricks—" Samantha held up both palms to show her hands were empty, then flipped her wrists and presented two fans of cards. "Don't be so certain that I'm not just awfully good at sleight of hand. The price for real magic is steep, remember?"

She placed the cards on the table in a neat stack and peeled down one of her elbow-high gloves. The exposed flesh was branded with a scattering of small tattoos. They were the junkie-scar reminders of all the spells Samantha Van Ayers had ever cast. The marks were bizarre: glyphs like the ones she'd transcribed from the key and secret words in languages that had been lost long before the destruction of Babel's tower. Some were black, but many were rendered in more striking colors. The tattoos crawled restlessly across her pale skin, colliding in slow motion, merging into gruesome shapes and obscene silhouettes before separating again.

They were not painful. If anything, the look on Samantha's face as she watched them creep across her forearm betrayed her pleasure. That was the danger of true magic: it was as addictive as any drug.

Samantha pulled up the glove. "Turning people into monsters is only a side effect of the enchantment. The bastard who created the keys is passing the spells' cost on to his marks. He swipes their dreams, and their humanity powers the magic that allows the theft. Whoever is doing this is potent and ruthless."

"That won't save him from me," the Corpse said. "Nothing will."

"Try to remember that there are other ways to fix things than guns and bombs."

"You don't get to lecture me, not while you're safe in here instead of helping me fight the cause of this madness."

"Lay off," Samantha snapped. "Just because the lobby's not choked with dead bodies doesn't mean I'm not doing my part."

The Corpse turned to go. Samantha exhaled, recovering her calm, and laid a hand on his shoulder. "Wait. Here's your fortune." She moved to flip over the top card of the deck she'd placed on the table, but fumbled slightly. Then, with a slight, embarrassed smile, she turned over the ten of hearts. "Well, well. It means good luck, Tris."

Samantha slipped the card into the pocket of the crimefighter's ragged coat and watched him disappear into the theater. Only when he was gone did she drop the card that had been atop the deck, the one she'd started to reveal before faking a fumble and palming it.

Pharos had been correct. The ace of spades was the Corpse's card.

— 3 —

## THE HOUSE OF DREAMS

The building at the corner of Vine and Vedder had been mistaken for lucky at one time. The Great Chicago Fire had singed its mansard roof and charred its tower, but its odd, oblong windows watched intact as the neighboring structures burned. When the conflagration was finally contained, the recently completed three-story home had no neighbors for a few blocks to the west and for half a mile to the east, all the way to Lake Michigan. The desolation stretched much farther than that to the north and south. Stories circulated about angels emerging from the tower to extinguish the threatening flames. No one could swear to having witnessed the miracle firsthand, though even the most ardent skeptics admitted that a strange wind—notable even in the Windy City—could sometimes be felt hissing through the hallways and around the yard.

The building became a symbol of defiant hope on the North Side. The locals all predicted a great destiny for it.

Then the people and businesses inhabiting the place failed, one after another, in increasingly public and disturbing fashion. For four decades, wealthy families slid into poverty and the noblest of undertakings soured into scams. After a raid in 1911 revealed the horrors inside the Newsboys and Bootblacks Home that had taken up residence there, the Northsiders finally gave up on the building at the corner of Vine and Vedder. Those who had once believed the tales of angels began to cross the street rather than pass through its shadow. A succession of sleazy tenants, culminating in the opium den that opened there late in 1926, only strengthened their loathing. The local wisdom now had it that whatever good fortune the place would ever possess had been mortgaged to save it from the flames.

"Kang Hai would never set up a hop joint here," whispered the tong enforcer crouched in the alley across from the house. He watched a sailor shuffle unsteadily up the walkway and the steps to the front porch; like the three other junkies who had arrived since nightfall, the sailor found the route challenging. A hulking guard opened the front door to assess the would-be customer. The thug stood well over six feet tall. He wore a wide-sleeved tunic and had a bandana tied over the lower part of his face like a cheap stick-up man or a train robber from an old Tom Mix two-reeler. He eyed the silver key the sailor presented before stepping aside to admit him.

As the door thudded shut, the enforcer scowled, then scanned the alley for something unseen. "Do you feel that wind? It's the breath of Hell."

The figure lurking behind him in the darkness shifted slightly. The horrors perpetrated upon him by Drucci's doctors had dulled the Corpse's senses, but from time to time since they'd taken up their position across from the house he'd felt the touch of chill, unseen fingers. They reached through the hot summer night to trace the scars on his face and the puckered reminders of old bullet wounds on his arms and chest. "Whatever it is, it's not from Hell," the Corpse said. "It's cold."

"Some of the chambers in Mingfu are frozen," said the enforcer. "Even Dante knew that about the Dark Mansion."

"So this is a gateway to Hell. It won't be the first I've walked through. If you're afraid, leave."

The enforcer slipped a silver-bladed hatchet from his belt and twirled it with surprising deftness, considering the two missing fingers on his right hand. "I gave Kang Hai my word to aid you in closing down this rat hole, *shi*. I am afraid, but with me, honor always conquers fear."

"We'll see about that," the Corpse replied. He checked the satchel slung over his shoulder and unholstered his guns. "We've been staking the place out long enough. There's only the one guard at the front door and the other entrances are boarded up. The front's our best way in."

The crimefighter watched the tong hatchetman creep across the street to the cover of the wooden fence surrounding the house. He didn't trust the enforcer. He'd only accepted his presence as a necessary condition for Kang Hai's cooperation in identifying the opium den connected to the silver keys. The Chinese mastermind, known as the Celestial Executioner and the Hand of a Thousand Rings in the secret circles of international crime, was a force to be reckoned with around the globe, though Capone and Moran and the other prominent Chicago gang bosses were too narrow-minded to think a mere "oriental" could challenge them in their own city. Kang Hai was content to let them wallow in that delusion. It made conducting business far easier than it would have been, had they recognized his true status.

Kang's reaction to the silver keys ruled him out as their creator; when the Corpse presented them, he reared back in obvious and uncharacteristic fear. The strength of that revulsion told the Corpse everything he needed to know about the gravity of the threat, too. Fortunately, the crimelord had a good idea which den utilized the keys as passes—the proprietors could not get opium in Chicago, save through his network—but he had not known about their use of magic. "Those keys are the tools of madmen or fools," Kang Hai said. "You are a suitable force to contend with representatives of either of those classes. Allow me to direct you to their doorstep."

Kang would not discuss the keys further and brusquely ordered one of his men to accompany the Corpse in the assault on the opium den. The crimefighter recognized the enforcer assigned to him by his missing fingers, which he'd blown off the man's hand himself the previous summer, during a skirmish at a tong stronghold.

As the Corpse crossed the street to join the hatchetman at the fence, he wondered if it wouldn't be simpler just to finish him off then and there. They had located the den, and the enforcer might betray him during the fight. The killer was living on borrowed time after his unlikely escape from the stronghold raid anyway. Only the arrival of Kang Hai's clockwork spiders had prevented the Corpse from adding him to the body count at the tong lair, one more deserving casualty in his war on corruption and chaos.

The Corpse tightened his grip on his automatics, but didn't fire. It wasn't Samantha's admonitions about violence that caused him to hesitate, though; he found himself admitting, albeit grudgingly, that the tong enforcer might still prove of some use in the assault. The Corpse let go of his desire to kill the man. As he did, the keys in his jacket pocket, trapped within a folded ten of hearts, pulsed with blue light.

When he saw the eerie radiance, the Corpse said, "We have to take the fight to them now. Whatever is holed up inside this place knows I'm here."

They vaulted the fence and sprinted across the small yard. The hatchetman silently veered off to leap onto the long, railed porch. Keeping the enforcer in his sights the whole time, the Corpse cut toward the walkway as if he were going to charge right up to the front door. When he reached the lowest steps to the porch he stopped abruptly, then rolled to his left—just before the door flew open and the masked guard squeezed the trigger of the Tommy gun clutched in his hands. Bullets chewed up the ground where the crimefighter had been standing an instant before.

The guard stalked onto the porch, the black barrel of the machine gun jutting before him. He leveled the gun to fire a burst into the scraggly, heat-wilted bushes alongside the path, but a hatchet shattered his left wrist and sent the Tommy gun clattering away from him, down the steps. The guard turned to see Kang Hai's minion grip his hatchet to strike again. This time the enforcer aimed for the wicked scar that ran from the man's hairline down between his eyes. Just before the blade struck, the masked thug raised his left arm, hand dangling on its savaged wrist, to check the blow. The blade skinned away part of the tunic's wide sleeve before lodging in the forearm with the wet thud of metal biting into meat and bone.

The wounded hop joint guard laughed.

At least that's what the bizarre, rolling cough coming from behind the bandana mask sounded like to the enforcer as he tried to wrench the hatchet free. Through the rent in the sleeve, he could see where the blade was stuck. The flesh there was dark, swollen, and matted with uneven patches of thick hair. The wound did not bleed. The hatchetman had assumed the tunic was intended to ape the garb of the Chinese who served in Kang Hai's opium dens. He knew now that the loose-fitting garment was meant to conceal the guard's hideousness.

The enforcer lashed out with an open hand in a tiger claw strike to the jaw. The guard's head snapped back and the bandana came away, revealing a face with no nose and a mouth turned completely sideways. The maw trailed off into the scar that bisected his forehead, a scar that strained in time with the guard's gibbering laugh, as if it were trying to open. The enforcer gasped and retreated a step.

The loud clack of the Tommy gun's bolt was the only warning the hatchetman had before the Corpse opened fire from the foot of the stairs with the guard's own lost weapon. The enforcer dropped flat onto the weathered wooden porch; it was a similar move to the one that had saved him from the Corpse a year earlier. The machine gun barrage slashed the air above him and sent the monstrous thug, axe still buried in his forearm, reeling through the door. Picking himself up, the enforcer drew a knife and rushed into the house.

The Corpse marched up the steps and into the entry hall. Inside the house at the corner of Vine and Vedder, all was chaos. Opium smoke swirled in the cold draft that hissed from the upper floors and snaked through the halls. Shouts of alarm and confusion mingled with the groans and sighs and laughter from the hopheads too lost in a drugged stupor to recognize what was going on around them. A few of the more lucid patrons thought to escape, but retreated back into the warren of filthy rooms when they saw the Corpse standing sentry at the front door. The remains of the guard lay scattered and beheaded at his feet. The tong enforcer was nowhere to be seen.

From the second floor landing came the sound of breaking glass and splintering wood, then a frantic, frightened plea in Chinese. The enforcer's silver hatchet sailed over the balcony rail and spun down into the entry hall a moment before the thing appeared. It was the next stage of the metamorphosis that had twisted Sean Halloran and the hop joint guard: a huge, shaggy creature with a nightmarish head gaping from crown to chin with a vertical, snaggle-fanged mouth. Its bulging forearms ended in hands spiked with claws. In one of these it held the limp form of the tong enforcer. It turned its head to regard the Corpse with one eye, like a bird sizing up an insect, then contorted its mouth in a noiseless snarl.

The Corpse opened up with the Tommy gun, filling the night with Chicago lightning. The thing staggered back from the rail. Quickly the Corpse drew a gas mask from his satchel. He fitted it with practiced speed, a legacy of his time in the trenches of France, then took a small bomb and lobbed it onto the second-floor landing. A yellow-green cloud mushroomed up before being warped into flowing, fantastic shapes by the wind. Wreathed in the searing gas, the thing screamed silently. It clutched at its throat and eyes before collapsing on the stairs. The Corpse emptied the machine gun into its twitching form.

After locking the front door and jamming the security bolts as best he could, the Corpse made his way through the lower floor of the opium den, lobbing bombs as he went. The rooms had been parlors and libraries at one time, with bright wallpaper, ornate cornices, and gaudily patterned tin ceilings. Now all was stained and grubby. Filthy cots lined the walls. Lamps and pipes and other junkie debris littered the floors. The Corpse didn't encounter any more of the larger creatures here, just addicts and small-time hoods choking on the opium smoke and chlorine gas. Pain contorted their faces, though whether from the poison or the transformation taking hold of the silver key holders as their dreams fled, the crimefighter could not tell.

Wraithlike in the deadly, shifting fog, the Corpse moved from room to room. He ran out of maggots to mark the bodies long before his grim work was done.

## — 4 —
### STRANGE GEOMETRIES

The wind grew colder and more insistent as the Corpse climbed the stairs to the second floor and then the third. By the time he reached the steep stairwell that led to the tower, its drone drowned out the thud of his shoes on the wooden steps and the rasp of his breath in the gas mask. The wind tugged at the peeling wallpaper, making the edges flap like fingers gesturing for the intruder to retreat. The motion drew his eye, but his gaze lingered on something else on the wall: the vine pattern on the paper. The leaves and stems tangled with numbers and arcane symbols, then became them. The design expanded to show the equations they'd found on the keys, the components of Pharos's "complicated formulae."

When he looked away from the wall, the Corpse was no longer on the stairway to the tower room. He stood upon the steps leading into a massive stone structure. The air was clear here, swept clean of smoke and poison by the winds, so he tore off his mask and gazed up. Ancient, cyclopean blocks towered above him to form something like a monastery, the only feature on a vast and cold desert plateau that stretched for miles in every direction. The sands whirled and trembled beneath a sky filled with stars by which no human sailor would ever navigate. The Corpse felt the draw of the vastness overhead. It promised oblivion, if only he would retreat into its embrace, while the stone path ahead beckoned him to a very different sort of doom: equally certain, but finite and particular.

He took a step forward.

The Corpse stood once more on the tower stairs. With his next step the prehistoric monastery and the high desert wastes returned. They were, in turn, replaced by the wooden treads and the papered walls with their expansive grid of equations. It continued like this with mystifying irregularity, his surroundings stuttering in and out of reality, ghostly one moment, solid the next. Eventually, the distinctions between the places blurred until the crimefighter pushed ahead through both worlds and neither.

At last the Corpse came to the heart of the monastery-tower. There, upon a simple limestone throne, sat a tall, thin man garbed in tattered yellow robes of state. The room around him wavered between cavernous hall and cramped attic, sometimes mixing the two in strange configurations. The figure remained more fixed; he was phantasmal, but he never completely vanished. A mask of pallid yellow silk covered his face. Now and then the Corpse could glimpse features behind it—piercing brown eyes, a forehead creased in intense concentration. At other times the mask hung on empty air. The silk did not cling to the wearer, but it shifted with the movement of his lips, even when there seemed to be no lips behind it.

"This faltering between places is maddening, I know," the man said. A wisp of blue light streaked in from somewhere. It zigzagged, changing directions to counter the buffeting wind, then struck him in the chest. He gasped appreciatively. "Ah! The turmoil will end soon enough, though. That's your purpose here. It's why I have allowed you to reach me."

The Corpse drew his twin automatics. Five shots rang out, but the bullets never reached their target. They passed through the robed figure and ricocheted off the limestone throne.

"You're only wasting ammunition," said the man. "Controlling where I am not was the first skill I mastered when I took the throne. Controlling where I am has been more of a challenge. So I am not yet fully manifested here. By the by, you should be kneeling. You're in the presence of a king."

"That's the bunk," the Corpse said. "You're a professor who wrote a book about geometry."

"Actually, the mathematical truths derived from the interplay of geometry and geography, especially the geography of—well, of things and places you won't understand. If that is the work to which you are referring, I am indeed its author." Robert Eddison Beckford, Doctor of Philosophy, leaned forward on the throne. His head wove from side to side in a curiously reptilian fashion as he studied the Corpse. "I must admit that your apparent astuteness is something of a surprise, given your costume and the way you blundered in here. The formula on the keys led you to my identity, I suppose. You're a marginally skilled detective—or you had help figuring everything out."

"All that matters is that I'm here to end this."

"Yes, yes. I said as much earlier." Another blue wisp pierced Beckford's chest and he paused, shuddering with pleasure. In that moment, he appeared more solid. "I also said you should kneel. I know that royalty 'consists not in vain pomp,' but there is a point to it this time, I assure you."

He gestured and a massive paw, nearly three feet in width, emerged from an unseen angle in the room, a corner that should not have been there. It slammed down on the Corpse, crushing him to his knees. The pressure diminished as the thing phased out, and the crimefighter looked back to see its ghostly form standing above him, merged with the walls and ceiling joists of the tower room. It was a giant, stoop-shouldered beast with a shaggy coat and bifurcated forearms, each branch ending in a paw. Its head resembled nothing so much as a Venus flytrap; it was split almost from front to back by a wickedly fanged mouth. Bulbous, unblinking eyes protruded on stalks from either side of the maw. They were fixed on the Corpse with hungry intensity.

"It's called a gug," Beckford said. "You encountered their warped reflections downstairs, imitations created when I use the keys to appropriate enough of someone's dreams. Like those imitations, the originals do my bidding. They have done so ever since I came upon this mask and robe abandoned on the throne and dared put them on."

The Corpse flexed his shoulders, pushing up against the gug's bulk. The thing was not pressing down. Rather, it had one barrel-sized paw poised over him as a precaution. It wouldn't be much of a challenge for the monstrous creature to keep him in check, at least when it was substantial. The experiments perpetrated upon the Corpse by Drucci's doctors had left him physically weaker than most men. He was, however, confident that he could outsmart or outmaneuver the beast—and its master. "You're supposed to be dead," the Corpse said to Beckford, then flexed again and began counting off the time before the pressure on his shoulders faded.

"Death, as you understand the concept, was never my fate, no matter what that butcher Holmes intended when he assaulted me inside that labyrinthine 'castle' of his. After the attack I found myself on this plateau. A less learned man might mistake the place for one of the more desolate corners of the Christian afterlife." Beckford's voice took on a smug, pedantic tone. "But I recognized its true nature instantly. It is nowhere less than the destination for which I had prepared myself. A lost location I had predicted in my book, if you read it carefully enough and grasp its more subtle truths. What occurred may appear supernatural to someone ignorant of higher mathematics, but I assure you: it was through reason and science that I escaped my supposed doom, and it is through reason and science that I will make my way back to the world."

The Corpse cursed under his breath. The way the gug appeared and disappeared was random; he couldn't plot anything based on the pattern. There had to be something else, though, some vulnerability he could exploit. The mask, perhaps. Beckford had said something about it giving him control over the monsters. He'd just need time to figure a way to get his hands on it—if it ever became solid enough for him to get his hands on.

"Hopheads and sharpsters?" the crimefighter spat. "They're the foundation for your scheme?"

"Not them. It is their hopes and aspirations, and then their unconscious cerebrations that I claim to complete the equation that will stabilize the lattice and fully bridge the worlds. Your dreams, too. You were carrying the keys attuned to me, so I took that little fantasy you had of destroying the Chinaman after you abandoned it. True, it had a bitterness the opium reveries lack, but it was vivid and I could tell you had many more like it. Soon, I'll claim those dreams, too."

Bowing his head to hide his movement, the Corpse slipped his hand into his jacket pocket. He pushed aside the folded playing card and withdrew the two silver keys. He gripped them so the pins protruded between the closed fingers of his left fist, the spikes of a makeshift knuckleduster. There was no expression on his dead man's face to suggest his self-satisfaction as he looked back up. He knew if he'd kept Beckford talking long enough he would get something to work with, and now he had it.

"If you think you're taking anything from me, you're the one who's dreaming," the Corpse growled.

The crimefighter surged forward, away from the momentarily non-corporeal gug. He would have preferred to time the attack so it coincided with a stolen dream striking Beckford, so his target might be more solid, but the unpredictable state of his monstrous guardian made that all but impossible. The keys, though, were weapons he could use even if Beckford were still a phantom. They were attuned to him; Beckford had said so himself. As the Corpse scrambled toward the man on the throne, he visualized how it would play out: drive the keys into Beckford's eyes, gouge them out, then snatch the mask off his face, breaking his hold over the creatures—

Beckford swiped a hand through the air. The Corpse collapsed like a cow brained with a slaughterhouse sledgehammer.

"Quite satisfactory," Beckford said as he stood over the stunned and gasping vigilante. He studied the blue ember in his palm. The light from the stolen aspiration painted the pallid yellow silk of the mask a sickly hue. He absorbed the ember into his hand, and the mask smiled. "Yes, quite satisfactory. I inferred that humbling you might inspire visions of revenge, ones even fresher than your desire to kill the Chinaman. I must say, newly minted hopes are far more satisfying than the stale old things I have been consuming up to this point. I am glad I tested the hypothesis. But now it's time to complete the equation."

Beckford inscribed an arcane sign into the air with his fingertips. His movements were unlike Pharos's exaggerated stage magic pantomime. Rather, they resembled the subtle gestures of Samantha van Ayers when she cast a spell, if colder and more precise, as if the professor were writing a formula on a chalkboard. Another hope tore free from the Corpse, then another. Each theft was a scalpel slash.

The vigilante gritted his teeth and tried to push himself to his feet. He managed to struggle only to his knees. As more and more blue light bled from him, he forced himself to open his left hand. The two keys he had thought to wield as weapons dropped to the floor, one thudding on wood, the other pinging off stone. Ridding himself of them did nothing to slow the assault. He was so deep in the matrix of equations and mystical symbols inscribed on the tower walls, so close to the ancient limestone throne, the keys were no longer necessary. Beckford could plunder the dreams directly from his psyche.

The first to be taken were conscious hopes, like the casual plans he'd imagined for killing the tong soldiers guarding Kang Hai at his office or the petty hoods who'd conspired with Sean Halloran. As these left him, the Corpse's face grew even more gaunt. His flesh, already pale and tinged blue like a drowned man's, lost whatever traces of living color had clung to it. His bones twisted, and when he opened his mouth to scream, he felt something splinter in his skull. Despite the pain, the Corpse resisted. Each dream had to be pulled from him as if it were his last.

It was a losing battle. The stolen wisps made Beckford stronger and more substantial. "Interesting," he said and cocked his head. "These dreams have an odd—" He paused as a spasm shot through his form, stiffening his arms and making his head jerk back. "They have an odd texture," he said when he'd recovered. "A harshness I've not encountered elsewhere." A sly smile spread across the yellow silk mask.

The Corpse could feel Beckford digging relentlessly for deeper desires. The vigilante fought to save the aspirations of Tristram Holt, the man he'd been before the nightmare experiments, but it was like trying to catch smoke with frozen hands. Fleeting images of the happy life he'd hoped to share with his fiancée, Angela Burton, and the noble career he'd envisioned for himself as a lawyer flickered between the white flashes of torment searing his brain. He clutched at them but they slipped away, to be replaced by other secret desires flitting in his mind's eye—to return from the war a decorated hero, to turn the acting he'd done in college into a life on the stage, to save Samantha from the dark lure of magic he knew would destroy her one day. Then they, too, vanished.

Beckford could feel the weight of each dream and taste its value as he gathered them. The personal aspirations were less fully formed than he'd expected, little more than vivid fragments. By the time he'd got to this level with the thugs who carried the silver keys, he'd uncovered elaborate, if predictable fantasies of riches and women. Not so with the vigilante. The only dreams that were wholly realized in him were visions of justice. And these had uncomfortably sharp edges. Beckford could not help but flinch as he took them in.

Though the Corpse could scarcely recognize himself, mentally or physically, he sensed that discomfort. It reached him on the dreams streaming from him to Beckford like an impulse traveling along a nerve. He stopped resisting.

The Corpse's remaining conscious hopes poured into Beckford, and when they were gone, the gates of his unconscious slammed open. The visions of justice that surged forth now were not just bloody, but terrifying. No mercy tempered them. They were grand and vibrant, magnificent nightscapes of unyielding, ruthless order, all the more substantive because they had been forged in the fires of a will strong enough to transform them into actions. The piles of bodies in his deepest dreams were not different from the ones he'd actually created in Chicago, only larger. Upon the savaged remains of Drucci's doctors and the other foes he'd destroyed, from armored simian assassins and demon-ridden cartoonists to a rogues gallery of more mundane thieves and murderers, were heaped those of the adversaries he had not yet destroyed: Al Capone and "Bugs" Moran, Kang Hai and Robert Beckford. His enemies were legion, and the details of their deaths were stunning and grotesque. With each new butchery, each new shocking masterpiece of carnage, maggots pooled to mark the Corpse's triumph, until the writhing mass spread beyond Chicago to blanket the country and then the globe.

The horrible dreams overwhelmed Beckford. There were too many of them and they were too aggressive. Even when he could absorb one, it cut him up inside like he'd swallowed broken glass. The ones he could not contain filled the room, a tumbling swarm of razor-winged bats that tore into everything in its path, in either world. The dreams notched stone and wood alike, slashed Beckford and the warped form of the Corpse writhing before the throne. The gug reeled back. Its taloned paw lay on the floor, severed and oozing purple gore. It looked to Beckford for a command in the moments before the whirlwind sliced it apart. The professor was gesturing wildly in the air, alternately trying to break contact with the Corpse's psyche and defend himself from the swarming dreams. It was no use. Beckford had not factored such savage fantasies into his equations, and now he was undone by his broken calculus.

The Corpse's dreams slashed open the would-be king from within and from without before returning to their father. As they flowed into him, the Corpse found his form and senses returning. He was lifted up and up, until he could see the entire plateau—and the vast, variegated geography of wasteland and metropolis, nowhere and everywhere, that spread out below and beyond the plateau. Through pain-bleared eyes, he watched the rest of the stolen dreams escaping Beckford's body through the thousand cuts, all limned in blue light. The dreams belonging to those victims still alive vanished through the walls of the house and streaked out into the Chicago night. The dreams of the dead rained down upon the cold desert sands and, carried by the winds, out across the rest of the Dreamlands. The tattered remnants of Robert Beckford went with them. Naked and screaming, he plummeted over the plateau's edge and vanished between the soaring towers that marked the city of the gugs, where the cursed and hideous giants wait to feast upon lost shades and wayward dreamers.

The Corpse found his consciousness snagged by a silent summons and pulled down once more to the monastery. There, the royal raiments Beckford had worn danced in the air, spinning and diving, tossed about on the claws of the whirlwind. The patterns they wove were hypnotic, and the Corpse stood watching them, transfixed. Then, at last, their dance ended and they settled back on to the throne to await their next claimant.

An overwhelming dread blossomed in the Corpse's chest and spread its tendrils throughout his body. Before it settled to the throne, the mask had hung still in the chill darkness for just a moment. And in that moment, a crooked smile quirked the mask, though no face lurked behind the pallid yellow silk.

The Corpse saw the awful truth then, and wondered how he had missed it before. The mask was the king, he realized with growing horror, not anyone who wore it. They were merely puppets. Beckford had been a fool to think such a thing could be wielded in the service of reason and science.

The pandemoniac chorus that was the wind screaming across the wastes yowled and gibbered its agreement as the mask and the throne and the prehistoric monastery receded, leaving the Corpse alone in the still, silent tower room.

The building at the corner of Vine and Vedder burned to the ground that night. It went up with preternatural speed, as if the Great Fire had reached across the decades to claim its long-denied prize. No stories circulated about angels emerging from the tower to extinguish the destroying flames, though a few of the neighbors who came to watch the conflagration swore that a dark-winged figure had leaped from one of the odd, oblong windows on the second story just before the building collapsed. No one was close enough to identify him—they'd been kept at a respectful distance by the gunfire and explosions that rocked the street shortly before fire stabbed up through the mansard roof—but even the most ardent skeptics admitted that the house's spectacularly violent end and the tales about the strange things found later in its ashes left little doubt as to his identity.

The Corpse had returned to Chicago.

The city trembled as he stalked through its shadows, intent on making his dreams a reality.

# — TRANSPLANT SPECIALIST —
## Sarah Goslee

*What is the heart of a town? In Connecticut, a single oak formed the heart not only of a town but of an entire state. The white oak tree that grew in what is now Hanford, Connecticut was such a powerful symbol of strength and independence that after it fell it was made into chairs for the heads of the Connecticut government. The tree has fallen, but the power of its memory remains.*

*The Connecticut Charter Oak was a white oak that was first described in writing by Dutch explorer Adrian Block in 1614. Local Native Americans planted the oak when they settled the area, long before Block first laid eyes on the tree. By studying the size of leaves of the tree, they could determine the best times to plant corn. The tree grew in what is now the town of Hanford.*

*In 1662, the General Court of Connecticut won a charter from King Charles II. This charter set the boundaries of the colony and gave the colony a degree of independence. Twenty-five years later, James II wanted tighter control over the colonies. He sent an armed force into Hanford to retrieve the charter. According to local legend, Captain Joseph Wadsworth spirited the charter away and hid it in the trunk of the oak.*

*The Charter Oak was so beloved that when it fell (during a windstorm in 1856), a marching band played funeral dirges at the site and the bells of Hanford rang at sunset in tribute. Today a memorial stands where the tree once stood, and the oak has passed into state lore. Wood from the oak was used to make the desk of the Connecticut Governor and chairs for the Speaker of the House of Representatives and the President of the Senate. Today a forest of white oaks grows from the acorns of the Charter Oak.*

Lizzy Alexander, Transplant Specialist, printed in stark black type on heavy cream cardstock, followed by a suitably generic email address. Nice. I checked my bag, turning out its many pockets. I found one last card printed with Elizabeth McGillivray and flipped it into the fireplace to join its companions. It wouldn't do to hand the mayor the wrong card.

The mayor of the shithole I was heading to wanted to convince people it wasn't a shithole, maybe get his town on one of those "Best Places to Live" lists. Here's a secret: those lists are rigged. Nine out of ten of those "best" towns? I put them there, and the tenth I just haven't bumped off the list yet.

I slung my bag over my shoulder, then picked up the leather-covered case holding my stock-in-trade. The silver tracery was getting worn; I needed to touch it up when I got home. I didn't want any spirits seeping out.

A boring three-hour drive was capped off by crossing the entire town to get to the mayor's office, one boring strip mall and cookie-cutter subdivision after another. Totally generic, and just the kind of place I most hated. A job was a job, though.

The mayor, Bob Smith or John Jones or something like that, was every bit as characterless as his town. Gray suit, expensive haircut, utterly bland. Only a silver and onyx ring on his right hand betrayed any evidence of personality.

"Ms. Alexander, it's a pleasure to finally meet you in person." He offered me coffee; I took it to be polite. I wanted to get this over with and get out of Podunkville.

"Mr. Mayor, the pleasure is all mine." I placed my case on his desk, but didn't open it. "I have here the genius loci of a town in New England, collected from the centuries-old oak in the town square. Transplanting it here will give your town the heart of a long-established and well-loved village." The Massachusetts town I'd taken it from would be a cold and unfriendly place for years, until its spirit started to re-form from the good will of its inhabitants, assuming they had any left. Not my problem: they hadn't hired me.

Smith reached for my case. "It's in here, isn't it?"

"Please don't. If you accidentally release the spirit before I install it, I will still expect payment." He pulled his fingers back as if burned. "Where do you want it?" I pulled out a map. "Not the geographic center, but the socio-cultural center. What are the town landmarks, the sites that people appreciate?" Assuming this shithole had any, that is.

Jones drew a circle on the map. "This is the old center of town. It's kind of run-down now, but I expect an urban renewal project to begin shortly." Smith smirked. "You should find something suitable there."

"You're not coming with me?" Usually the purchaser wanted to see the planting, even though nothing would be visible to anyone but me. It only took me a couple minutes to root a spirit, but I used a long, complicated ceremony with chanting and incense to keep the customer satisfied.

"I'm afraid not. I have an important meeting shortly. You can handle this without me, can't you?" He nudged my coffee cup towards me.

"Of course," I replied, and drank some of the coffee. I noticed a faintly off taste just before my head started to spin. I grabbed for SmithJones's desk to keep from falling over, but slid to the floor, unable to remember which way was up and which down. I could see a dust bunny under the desk and the mayor's feet, in gray shoes perfectly matched to his suit.

I tried to lever myself up, but couldn't move my arms or legs. His voice sounded anything but gray as he called into the outer office, "She's out."

The clatter of heels announced his secretary. When she bent down to touch my face, I saw a silver and onyx ring matching the mayor's. "Well done," she said.

"I didn't think she was going to drink the coffee," he replied.

"There's always a Plan B, but not necessarily one she'd walk away from." Meaning I might? What did they intend? I shivered, and my legs actually quivered in response. Whatever was in my swig of coffee was already wearing off. "I know you can hear me. Be a good girl and we'll let you go. Who could you tell? Spirits, drugs… you'd sound mad." She grabbed my head and twisted it to face her. "So you'll behave."

The woman—certainly not his secretary—flipped open the case despite my wards. As the lid rose the genius loci resolved in my inner vision. She smiled. "Nice. Such a strong spirit will work even better than we planned." She sprayed something into the case. The rusty smell of blood mixed with bitter rue, and something spicy I couldn't place, the three together so strong they were more a taste than a smell. The spirit roiled and darkened; I'd never felt anything like it. "Look at that," she said. "A negative spirit. People will become more and more uneasy here, then run off in droves because they just can't stand living here one more minute."

"I can feel it already," Jones said, leaning in over the case beside her.

"It doesn't matter; it's not like we need to live here to drill for natural gas. We only need the land."

I'd heard enough. I couldn't quite move cohesively, but I could still do my job. I called the genius loci to me, and it came: right through both of them. They dropped, boneless. Human bodies didn't take well to extra spirits passing through, especially nasty black ones like this.

I pried myself off the floor, wobbling as I closed the case, genius safely inside. Reassuring to know a spirit that had been messed with could still be controlled. I stuffed the spray bottle in my bag. Its contents would come in very handy, especially if I could figure out what they were.

Time for new cards: Beth Livingston, at your service. Genii locorum, transplanted or cursed: double the business for me or twice the trouble for you.

# — THE GRAMADEVI'S LAMENT —
## Sunil Patel

*Sunil Patel's story "Gramadevi" is told from the viewpoint of the spirit that guards a village. Sunil learned about gramadevi's from his grandmother. She told him two things that were crucial for his story—gramadevi from other villages cannot talk to each other, and when a woman marries and leaves her village, she worships her new home's Gramadevi and no longer "belongs" to the gramadevi of her childhood.*

*The tradition of the gramadevi as practiced in the state of Orissa in Eastern India comes from a folk religion that predates Hinduism. In this belief system, a village is only possible when the goddess is felt in some location. Anything will serve as the location as long as it is specific (a tree or rock, for instance). This spot marks the boundary of the village. The gramadevi represents peace, order, justice, and protection. She is particularly careful to ensure that the village endures across generations; by making sure that people successfully procreate and that their children survive into adulthood.*

*In the Oriya culture, the village depends on the gramadevi, and she is always present and always female. Unlike more grandiosely supernatural deities, the gramadevi cares for her villagers in practical terms, and sometimes she is seen walking around the village in the form of an old woman. Villagers can communicate directly with her in their dreams. Periodically, a prophet called the kalisi manifests the gramadevi and makes predictions for the coming year.*

*The gramadevi brings health, but sometimes she brings sickness and death as well. In the Oriya tradition, illnesses and other disasters are seen as the will of the gramadevi.*

The pungent scent of corpses fills the air, anathema to human nostrils like yours. Though I have none, tonight I choose to be assailed by the smell. Underneath the rusty corrugated metal roof of R-53 lies Bhikhabhai, who once tended cattle. Flies gather around his thick mustache as they often plagued his cows' tails. His simple home is as empty as the rest of the village of Tuldara. The village is quiet but for the buzzing of flies and the occasional bay of a water buffalo. I could interpret it as a paean, but it is not the prayer

I have missed for decades. It was the people who believed in me, not the animals.

Let me tell you about Pooja.

Pooja had a laugh like the clinking of bottles, a toast before a wedding. Darker than any other child in the village, wearing the silliest T-shirts imported by her cousins in America, she was three feet of joy. As her father had been a sullen child, I presumed she took after her mother, whom I met as a radiant young woman, newly married and newly mine. Pooja's parents brought the girl to me many times, but it was five years until she came to on her own. Her eyes lit up at our first unsupervised encounter, whereas my eyes, carved into a small marble figurine with the contours of a face, could do nothing. Towering over me, she shouted, as if afraid her words would not reach me otherwise.

"Tulda-ma!" she said, mangling my name. "I had the ball and I wouldn't give Kinjal the ball and he said to give it and I didn't give it so he hit me in the nose and it hurt." She rubbed the crook in her nose, still sore. To my surprise, she asked nothing of me. No wish for revenge, no command to pester him with mosquitoes or poison his parents' crops. And then she ended with three words I had never heard before:

"Tame kem cho?"

How are you?

I am Tuldaramma. I am the gramadevi. I am the village spirit, the all-mother, the protector. I am malady and remedy, blight and blessing. In the pantheon of gods I am paramount, prayed to before all others. I am everything to these people. They are everything to me.

They were.

Pooja believed in me like no one else did. Her parents, devoted though they were, feared me, adorning me with turmeric and vermilion and bringing me betel leaves and garlands of flowers as tokens of appeasement.

"O Tuldaramma," they chanted, "you are great, and you are powerful. May you continue to offer the village your grace."

To their credit, they never asked after their own welfare. Only Pooja's. They prayed for rain in time of drought, as if I reigned over the weather. Though I knew that a well-nourished wheat field would benefit Pooja, I could do nothing. When rain came, however, their harvest was more bountiful than anyone else's.

But Pooja worshipped me with the true innocence of a child, dismissing my divinity and coming to me every morning with a new story to tell. Running into Satishmama's house and up the stairs to his hay loft during Hide and Seek. The vulgarities uttered by men discussing the latest cricket game. A curious kiss on the cheek from the boy who had once hit her.

"It was gross," she said, scrunching up her face.

A thousand stories she told me, yet I could tell her none myself.

Sometimes she would offer me a sip of her Limca. I was familiar with the drink, the sweetness of sugarcane melding with a flavor neither lemon nor lime, entirely of the world of man. I could taste what she tasted when I chose. She did not know that. To her, I was a white marble murti at the entrance to the village, lifeless as a stone, and she offered me soda.

Rows of houses stand across from each other, an exercise in contrasts. On the left, R-32 is a majestic abode with a welcoming porch swing hanging from a rusty metal chain, now forever still. Three stone columns stand in front, the green paint flaking away. Inside, the floor is made of marble. R-32 has a toilet, a luxury.

And across from it, R-55 is a tiny, narrow home with a television no bigger than a newborn child. Crosshatching logs form the foundation of the roof. The maid lies dead on the tiled floor of the kitchen, eternally heating the water for the morning shower. Outside, a hole in the ground for shit and piss marks the entrance to the fields.

My village lies on the spectrum between opulence and squalor. Perhaps yours does as well. Where have you come from? You will find that nothing here compares favorably to your home. Not anymore.

Yet I welcome you.

One day Pooja's parents came to me with a request. "O Tuldaramma, please keep Pooja from playing with the dogs." The stray, mangy dogs that wandered the village attracted the children with their sad eyes.

"They're so filthy and they carry diseases." I knew they were right, having cultivated the diseases myself, but I would never let my Pooja become infected.

Pooja was silent the next morning, as if she knew her parents had given me their side of the story. But she took a deep breath and launched into her tale. "I only hugged one dog."

Pooja did not know I dissuaded the dogs from howling and barking near her home at night, but she did know I saw all that went on in Tuldara. Her redundant confession was a sign of trust.

"It was dirty, and it didn't have a home. I have a home, and it didn't, and I wanted it to feel welcome." She leaned down and whispered a correction: "Him."

Although she had been initially hesitant, I heard in her voice the confidence that I would not judge her for her actions, not as her parents did. I could not scold her, not as her parents did.

Some days she brought the dog to me. His name was Kut-Kut.

I sit at the threshold of the village, a guardian. Everything within the borders of Tuldara is my entire world, and I remain just outside it, an observer and caretaker. My reach extends no further than the hazy demarcation dividing Tuldara from the rest of India, the rest of the world. I cannot see it. I cannot know it. I cannot speak to it. I know I must have many sisters and yet I have never spoken to one. What are their villages like? Surely more full of life than mine, now.

You stand now in the aura of Tuldara, having only begun to enter. Don't look behind you. My perception reaches as far as your sight, and I promise you are safe. Nothing is behind you. Come closer. Don't be afraid.

As Pooja grew older, she traded her Limca for Thums Up, the off-white, sweet lemon-lime for the dark, acidic cola. She still offered it to me, though I sensed it was in jest. She had begun to question, as children do in their teenage years. "How are you?" became "Are you?" I was. I was, and she was, but only one could offer proof of existence, a tangible effect on the world with a clear attribution.

"Tuldaramma," she said, "I don't know whether you're there."

It hurt to hear those words. I had heard them from so many children before, but hearing them from Pooja was different. I had convinced myself she would not say them.

"I am here," I could not say, "and I love you."

"I don't know why I'm telling you this," she said, looking at the ground, "but they bought me a new bicycle. It has a basket *and* a bell! I'm going to ring the bell all the time the way everyone honks their horn all the time." She tilted her head up, smiling at me with a glint in her eye. "Like it'll make them go faster."

She exaggerated her bell-ringing plans. Right before she left the village, she would stop ringing the bell, and as she crossed the threshold, she would ring it twice in quick succession. Just for me.

I am the dirt. I am the air. I am the darkness itself. I permeate every facet of Tuldara from the columns outside Bhulabhai's residence to Lalitaben's rotting corpse. I am every particle of dust, I am the quiet, I am the swing no longer creaking.

I am not the stars. The stars are their own realm.

The bark of a dog startles you. Pay him no mind. Kut-Kut merely yearns for his playmate, as I do. I kept him to keep me company.

Will you keep me company too? It has been so long since I have received any knowledge of the world beyond Tuldara. You can tell me so many things. Tell me about my sister. Tell me about the village that gave her life, the villagers that still thrive.

Tell me I have not been alone.

As she became a young adult, Pooja came to accept me into her heart once again, believing in me because she chose to, not because she had no choice. Her devotion felt stronger now, backed by such conviction. She never asked me for anything, even then. Perhaps she understood that her parents cared enough for her that she had my blessing, always. Or perhaps she sensed that I had desired a friend since before she was the merest flicker of an idea.

"Kinjal and I walked through the wheat fields today," she said. I knew, of course, having felt them pass through the long, yellow stalks, laughing and saying more than the words they spoke.

Hers, playfully defiant: "Short girl like me with hair like this?"

His, warmly confident: "No problem finding a husband."

She rode a scooter now, and she never wore a helmet. I could not protect her when she left the boundaries of Tuldara, and the road held deadly curves. Several of my people had fallen throughout the years. Yet I could tell her nothing. That reckless girl. Our love flowed in both directions but our dialogue only in one.

Your eyes narrow; your forehead creases. You also wear no helmet, despite coming down those curves on a motorcycle. Worry not, girl. Pooja did not die. That is not how she was taken from me.

His name was Ranjit. A bold, strapping young man, with a booming voice, a model suitor to any sensible mother. His family had been deemed compatible with her family, though I had no say in the matter. Pooja's parents had come to me, but, as their daughter often did, they spoke for their own benefit, aware that I knew nothing of this boy from another village. Likewise, my sister knew nothing of Pooja, and yet she conspired with this boy's parents, feeding them lies to steal my—

No, no, she could not have done so. She had no role in this.

Kinjal, too, had no say in the matter. Yet now he said nothing, curled up in Satishbhai's hay loft, staring at the unfeeling wood of the roof.

The people of Tuldara approved of this boy. They welcomed him into our village. Pooja accepted him. Not as she had accepted me as an adult but as she had as a child. Because it was the single option presented to her.

In the early morning before the village woke, she cried to me. She had not cried to me since she was a girl, and now as a woman she spoke to me in tears, a wordless monologue. What began as a paroxysm of grief gave way to controlled sobs, brave sniffles as she steeled her resolve.

Tears welled up in her eyes as she prayed to me one final time that evening. As he took her hand and led her past the boundaries of Tuldara, my connection to Pooja severed and I lamented that I was unable to cry.

The people of the village are mine from the first day they arrive. The men are mine forever. No matter where they go, no matter how far they venture, they may always return to me. Tuldara never leaves them. The women, however, remain mine only until the day a man takes them away.

A woman who leaves with a man no longer belongs to me: she belongs to the goddess of his village. Not all villages have a goddess; some have a god, and some have no one. But she will worship whomever he does. Our history is tossed away as she forges a new relationship, and I am no longer obliged to listen to her prayers. In truth, I cannot. Even our one-way communication would be a luxury.

You are not mine. I do not know you. You have come because you have heard the stories. You have left your home to witness this haunted village.

There are no ghosts here but me, I assure you. You, who are not mine. Not yet.

It was only one mosquito at first. Disease vectors fall under my domain, and I expressed my grief the only way I could. I awakened a single mosquito, made it malarial. I knew Pooja could not stay with me forever. The women always left. The men brought me new women, strangers. But centuries, millennia had passed, and I wished for a new arrangement. For the first time, someone had treated me not as a force of nature but as a confidante. The village had betrayed me by allowing her to leave.

Every morning that Pooja did not come to me and tell me a new story, I awakened a new mosquito.

Pooja's parents fell ill within a week, and they came to me, laid a garland in front of the murti, prayed for me to cure them of this malady. I had that power. But I chose not to use it. They could not take away my choice as they had Pooja's.

I felt their agony, however. The convulsions, the sudden coldness, the bursts of heat, the nausea, the crippling fatigue. I had no body, but they were my people and their pain was mine. I could not cry for that either.

I could not communicate with other villages, and so neither could the villagers. Although it was not my intention, my isolation was so strong that it carried over into their realm. The borders were sealed, fused shut by my pain. Pooja did not know what I had done to her home. To her family.

The bodies began to fall, and they continued to fall. Mercifully, they died in their own houses, with the exception of Sukhooben, whose habit of wandering the village unattended left her body in the middle of the road. Hers was the only one not safe from the crows.

I spared the buffaloes, the dogs, the crows. They had done me no wrong.

The stench of rot and feces grew, and I let it remain. I could preserve life and I could take life. I could also preserve death. This was what I had done, and I would wallow in it.

It bothers you as well. You hold your nose between two lithe fingers to keep the stench out, but it will not work. The odor is more than smell; it is miasma, a weight that hangs in the air. A colossal absence of life, loss in return for my loss.

You pull your hand from your face, and clarity comes over me. Your nose is familiar. Thin, with a crooked bridge. Your eyes have her sparkle as well. I have not seen those eyes in many years. I welcome their curious gaze.

She was happy, then. For all her protests, she made a life with that stranger, a life I could not witness. She begat life that begat life, and here you stand, a living memory of the reason for this village's demise.

You are so beautiful. You do not deserve to enter here. To be defiled by what I have done to your origin.

What have I done? It was foolish, spiteful. You are the last vestige of Tuldara, as I have destroyed its history and its future. I have profaned the name of gramadevi; no all-mother am I. The scriptures warn of the dangers of attachment. Perhaps I was meant to be a reminder. I served that purpose admirably.

Now I implore you not to cross the threshold. Tuldara is unsalvageable, as is its goddess. There is no place for you here. Behind this archway lies only death.

Please. No.

But my pleas do not reach you. Your silence has communicated more to me than I will ever be able to communicate to you. I have told my story but taught you nothing.

And so you step into Tuldara, across the line that Pooja once crossed.

And you are mine.

# — BEER AND PENNIES —
## Richard Dansky

*The Devil's Tramping Ground is a well-known spot in North Carolina. The spot is a barren circle located in the middle of the forest. For three hundred years, locals have claimed that that the Devil walks the perimeter of the circle every night, plotting ways to destroy humankind. This circle is said to be perfectly round, and is forty feet across. The Devil does his planning at night, and in the daytime leaves to carry out his plan. Some say the circle is bare simply because it's too close to the devil's malevolent self. Other say the ground is scorched because of the heat from the devil's cloven hooves.*

*Any spot of ground so frequently visited by the Devil must exhibit some sinister side effects. Officially, the circle is a camping ground, with a firepit in the center, but according to legend no one can spend the whole night in the circle. People who try to keep a vigil see something that they cannot describe, and they go insane. Dogs won't enter the circle, not even for a Scooby Snack. Any object placed in the circle is expelled from it by morning by invisible forces. Some say all this is due to an ancient Indian curse, and some claim it's the site of a UFO landing. But most people stick with the story of the Devil, who paces through the night thinking of horrible, horrible things.*

*As it happens, a number of people have found that the Devil's Tramping Ground may not live up to its centuries of hype. The circle has shrunk considerably since it's 40-foot days, and visitors frequently find litter in the circle that seems to have been left there let alone overnight. Dogs like the circle just fine. Perhaps there was never anything wrong with the circle. Or perhaps the Devil has moved on.*

*But stories like this have a life beyond fact. The image of the Devil pacing and muttering and plotting through the night is so much more resonant and horrifying and seductive than the image of people hanging out in a circle of dirt and drinking beer while telling scary stories. And if it is true that the Devil walks the woods of North Carolina, even if he only walks those woods some of the time…would you want to know? What's the price of truth?*

—◖●◗—

I t was a week after Jimmy died that I called up the Devil.

Waited for him to call himself up, truth be told. I wouldn't have known how to call up the Devil, save in the usual way: living a damn fool life and then dying. The lucky ones lived long enough to find Jesus before they grew too old for the revival to take. The unlucky wrapped themselves around trees or smeared themselves across embankments; they drowned swimming after that one beer they oughtn't have had, or used the gun in a lawman's hand for suicide.

So I'd been told, anyway. The folks I'd known went more for quiet desperation and slow disintegration, and the only devils in their lives wore their own skins.

Jimmy and I had gone out to the Devil's Tramping Ground on a Monday night, that being when it was less likely to be occupied by local kids sneaking cheap beers and huffing paint in the woods. It had a legend, the Tramping Ground did—nothing would grow there, and anything left on that bare patch of ground in the Carolina woods overnight would get tossed out by some invisible force by morning.

The older folks, they had another part to the story. They said it was the Devil who'd clear things out of that circle of dirt and sand. That he'd show up there 'round midnight when the mood took him, and walk round and round planning mischief for mankind. That's why nothing would grow there, they said. The Devil ground it all underfoot.

Jimmy thought this was all bullcrap, of course, and in those days I followed where Jimmy led. He had some idiot idea about making a video of us doing some kind of investigation of the place, then putting it up online. What was supposed to happen next, he never got around to telling me, but he seemed pretty sure it would make us famous and then rich, though maybe not in that order.

I went along with it because I always went along with what Jimmy did. It's what you did when Jimmy was around. He came up with some pants-on-head crazy idea, you spent half an hour arguing against it, and the next thing you knew you were walking backwards across a train trestle at midnight 'cause Jimmy thought it might be a hoot. And you swore you were never, ever going to go along with another one of Jimmy's idiot plans again.

At least, not until he cooked up the next one.

And the next one, and the one after that, until we stood on the edge of the clearing in the woods where the Devil's Tramping Ground lay.

It wasn't much to look at, truth be told. Just a flat sandy circle in a clearing in the woods. Burned out fire pit in the center, logs for sitting on around the edge. Nothing grew inside those logs, while outside scrubby grass and sickly weeds spread into the woods. Empty tallboys littered the place, a sure sign of recent visitation. But of the Devil, there was no sign.

"That's it?" I asked.

Jimmy nodded. "That's it. Just a circle of dirt people been telling stories about for a hundred years."

"We came all the way out here and it's just a circle of dirt?" I stalked after Jimmy, who did a fine job of ignoring me as he set up his camera.

"You can leave," he finally said. "Me, I'm going to sit here tonight with some thinking juice and the best technology Sony has to offer, and I'm gonna try and see if there's more to this here "circle-of-dirt" than just dirt. You can join me if you'd like." And he sat down on one of the logs, and patted the log beside him, and damned if I didn't sit down, too.

"Atta boy," he said when I did. "Now bust open the cooler and get a couple of beers. It's gonna be a long night."

And I did, and we sat and waited, and drank beers in the dark until morning.

Except, of course, neither of us made it 'til morning. I dropped off around four thirty, when Jimmy was already snoring like a drunk pig and the sky hadn't quite decided to start thinking about maybe getting light. We got woken up around ten, when a couple of tourists came walking up the trail hollering about how they thought they'd found the place. Jimmy checked the camera while I kept them occupied, but the look on his face told the story.

Nothing.

"Well, we got what we came for," I said after the tourists—two fat guys who said they were writers and their skinny, bored wives—had gone back to their car. "Now we going home?"

"Just for a little bit," Jimmy said, fiddling with the camera some more. "See this? Camera stopped recording for a couple of minutes right after we dropped off."

"Maybe that was 'cause we fell asleep."

He ignored me. "I wanna go home, get a wash and a change of clothes and some more beer, then come on back and try a little something."

I could feel the hackles on the back of my neck standing up. "Jimmy, something tells me this is gonna be a real bad idea."

Grinning, he shook his head. "Ain't gonna be nothing. Safe as can be. You'll see." And he headed back down the same trail to where we'd left Jimmy's truck, and I hurried to follow him.

We were back by five that night, plenty of time to set up the camera again and start a fire in that pit. We made supper and drank a few more beers, and then Jimmy got up to show me his bright idea.

Which, it turned, was a penny, and he tossed to me.

"What the hell is this?" I asked.

"A penny," he said. "Ain't you never seen one?"

"I've seen one, but I don't know why you got one here. You want penny slots, you got to go all the way to Cherokee."

"Naw," he said, and took the penny back. "You know the legend, right? Anything you leave in the circle overnight, the Devil tosses out. So I'm gonna leave this penny here, right near the fire, and I'm gonna leave the camera pointed at it all night. The Devil picks it up, we'll see it."

"You're an idiot," I said. "That's your big plan?"

He shrugged. "I figure a penny ain't a big thing. If the Devil does show, he won't be too put out movin' it."

I stared at him. "You serious? That's your plan? Sit here and wait for the Devil to bend down for loose change?"

"You got a better one?"

I grabbed another beer. "No. But if one comes along, I'm for it."

Jimmy laughed, and put down the penny, and picked himself up a beer.

It wasn't a tourist waking me up the next morning, it was Jimmy, and he was cussing up a storm.

"What is it?" I asked him.

"Well," he said, looking up from the camera, "the penny's gone but the camera's got nothing. All static from midnight on 'til about five, when a possum came in and ate what was left of your sandwich."

"Maybe the possum got the penny," I said, and stood up and stretched. "Or a bird picked it up 'cause it was shiny."

"Yeah, yeah." His attention went back to the camera. I was already up, so I took a stroll around the ring in hopes of nothing in particular. I could see already the penny was gone, and the only footprints I could spot belonged to Jimmy and the possum, respectively.

And then the sun busted through the clouds, and I thought I saw something gleam on one of the logs.

It was the penny. Only it wasn't on the log, it was in it, jammed halfway deep so that all you saw of old Abe Lincoln was his neck and shoulders. I bent down and looked at it. "Jimmy?" I said. "You might want to bring that camera over and look at this."

"Hmm?" But he saw what I was squatting down in front of, and got over there in a hurry.

"Shit," he said when he got close, drawing it out to about thirty seconds long and bringing the camera in for a close-up. "You want to try and pull that sucker out of there while I record it? This ought to be good."

So I reached in and I got a good grip, and I pulled. The penny didn't go nowhere. It was jammed in there real good. I tried again, wiggling it back and forth, but no dice. It wasn't going anywhere.

"Stuck?" Jimmy asked.

"Stuck," I said. "You want to try?"

We switched places, and he gave it a shot. There was a lot of cussing and bullshit excuse-making and Jimmy yelling "I think it's moving," but in the end he had to give up, too. We both just sat there on the ground, staring at it when we weren't staring at each other.

Finally, I said something. "Jimmy?"

"Yeah?"

"When you pulled on it..."

"Yeah?"

"Did that penny feel, I dunno, kind of warm to you?"

He looked away. "I thought that was maybe from you. Or the fire."

"Uh-uh." We sat for a minute. "Fire's been out a long time."

We sat there a while longer before he got up. "Right, I'm going home. Gonna get washed up, gonna try and figure out what the hell is wrong with the camera, and then I'm coming back. You with me?"

I stood. "I'm with you as far as going home, but that's about it. That," I said, and pointed to the penny, "ain't right. That's a warning, Jimmy. We been tolerated thus far. I ain't willing to push that no further."

"C'mon," he exploded. "Right now, all we got is a penny in a log. Coulda stuck that in there ourselves with a hammer. But we come back tonight—with coffee, not beer, so we don't fall asleep again—and we keep watching, and we're gonna get something awesome, man. We're gonna get the real deal."

"I don't want the real deal," I said, with a little heat. "I want to go home and sleep in my bed tonight and not come back here none because what you did last night got something riled up, and whatever you got planned tonight, well, I don't want to be a part of it."

"Fine," he said, and he was suddenly quiet. "Pick up the bottles. We're getting out of here. I'll come back here tonight alone."

And he did. He tried a couple more times to get me to go with him, but for once in my life I stayed firm and told him no. Around seven he finally gave up, cussing me out for being chickenshit, and drove off on his own. He didn't take coffee. He did take beer, and the camera, and a sleeping bag.

They found him in the morning, or at least that's what the cops told me. Found him ripped to shreds and hung up in the trees. Some of the meat was missing, which had the cops thinking wild animal attack, but his head was fifteen feet up a pine tree, and you tell me what kind of wild animal does that?

In any case, they'd brought back his camera, and they asked me lots of questions about what was on it. I told them everything I knew, which wasn't much—that we'd gone out there to shoot a video, that the camera maybe acted a little funny, and that I'd given up before the third night when he wanted to keep on going. I told 'em where I was that third night, and who could vouch for me, and everything I could think of that Jimmy had said to me and that I'd said to him before he left. After a while, they seemed satisfied, and got ready to go. They asked me not to leave the state, and told me they might have some other questions, but they didn't think I had nothing to do with it.

"Wild animal," one of the cops said. "Santers are back in this part of state, though ain't no one gonna admit it."

I didn't disagree with him. I didn't see why I should.

And a week later, I went back out to the Tramping Ground.

Dumb-ass idea, I know. The cops would probably want to know why I was going there. Maybe a scene of the crime thing, maybe they'd think I was looking for a souvenir.

Truth was, I was looking for an answer.

I pulled up along the side of the road, where that trail back and up into the woods started. There were no other cars there, just a line of yellow police tape cut in half and whipping back and forth in the breeze. That didn't seem like it ought to stop me, so I grabbed my bag off of the front seat and went walking up the path.

I left the car unlocked. If everything went well, I wouldn't be gone long. And if it went the way I thought it might, I wouldn't be needing the car no more anyhow.

The Tramping Ground was full of footprints, that much I could see when I got there. Police footprints, paramedic footprints, sightseer footprints, you name it. They'd done a good job of cleaning up Jimmy, but here and there you could still see a little splash of blood, or a little scrap of fabric from something that had maybe been his.

Fifteen feet up in the trees, they said. It made me want to puke.

Instead, I reached into the bag and brought out what was in there. It was a bottle of wine, red wine, the best I could afford. I smashed the neck against a rock and it split off, leaving a jagged top and expensive grape juice running down the sides.

"Here," I said, and poured out the wine into the circle. "Don't know if I'm doing this right. Don't know if I'm damning myself to Hell by doing this. But Devil, if you're there, this is me, inviting you. This me telling you I want some answers."

The last of the wine ran out onto the ground. I threw the bottle away into the woods. It hit a tree and smashed, and the pieces fell to the ground. Off in the distance, somebody's dog found something interesting and started barking up a storm.

Other than that, nothing.

"Well, damn," I said, and shook loose a cigarette from the pack I was carrying. Struck a light and settled into wait, and when I looked up he was there.

He was tall, but I'd expected that. For a moment he just stood there, and I took him in. He was dressed in a shabby black suit, cuffs frayed and shoes scuffed, mud on the heels and tie loosened past the first undone button of his sweat-stained white shirt. His face was dead-man pale, eyes bright and sharp under a shock of red hair which itself sat beneath a worn and battered felt hat. If he had horns, I couldn't see 'em, but perhaps that's what the hat was for. At least, that was my thinking.

"Your friend was a damn fool," he said, without waiting for preamble or question. "He was a damn fool and it killed him, and I'm hoping you're less of a damn fool than him." As he spoke, he began walking, long loping strides that took him around the perimeter of that circle of dead grass at a goodly clip.

I took a drag on my cigarette, then stubbed it out against the soggy bark of the log I was sitting on. "You're the Devil," I said. "What do I call you? Old Nick? Father of Lies? Lucifer?"

"You can call me the Devil," he said with a grunt. "I don't hold with being too familiar."

"The Devil it is," I agreed, and nodded to let him know I agreed with him. He didn't acknowledge the gesture, instead choosing to stump round that place where nothing grew, brow furrowed as if by some deep thought. "So, Mister Devil, what damnfool thing did my friend do to get himself killed?"

The Devil stopped. Looked at me, looked me up and down like a dog looking at a piece of steak that's fallen onto the kitchen floor. "Three nights," he said. "Three nights of being a pain in my ass. You were there for the first two," and he pointed an accusing finger. The nail, I could see, was charcoal black. "You were there for the first two, but you weren't stupid enough to cross the line. You just wanted to see, and seeing was enough for you. But he wanted to feel it, feel it for himself. Feel what it's like to have the Devil his own self lay hands on you and cast you out."

I stood, but cast my eyes down so they wouldn't meet his. You see things when you meet the Devil's eyes, or so Mama had always said. You see things it ain't right to see.

"So he pitched his tent in there?" I asked, and pointed to a spot where the dead turf looked to be torn up a little.

The Devil shook his head. "Didn't even bother to do that much. I think he figured it'd get all messed up, and he didn't want to deal with that none. He just laid his sleeping bag down and climbed in. Had a couple of beers while he was waiting to fall asleep, that cheap watered down Lite crap. Can't stand it myself, and then your idiot friend had to go and make things worse by leaving his damn cans in the circle. That's not the sort of thing I stand for."

I stepped closer to the edge of the circle. Maybe two feet of green and mud separated me from that patch of deadness where the Devil waited. He stood there, watching me, arms folded across his chest. He carried himself the way a tough man carried himself. Not a bully, mind you, but a lean, hard man used to working for a living and taking care of his business when he deemed it necessary to do so.

Then again, he was the Devil, with all that implied.

"That's what you killed him for, then? Littering?"

He glared at me. "That'd have been enough. I'm the Devil, boy. I'm the evil that's walked this land since the Flood receded and the dinosaurs died. A man looks at me funny, that's enough in my book for me to work some mojo on him."

A couple more steps took me right up to the line where the grass died. I was careful not to cross it. Didn't want to transgress the circle, for whatever that was worth. Didn't want to intrude on the Devil's space.

Hell, I didn't want to give him an excuse.

"So that's it," I said cautiously.

He fixed me with a stare, his head tilted to the side, like a bird's. "I didn't say that."

"But you—"

"Don't interrupt the Devil when he's talking, son. It's a bad habit, and it'll stunt your growth."

I shut up. He watched me shutting up for a minute, making sure I wasn't going to start yammering again, and then continued. "Tell you what. You want to know about your friend so bad, I'll make you a deal. Truth for truth. You tell me why you came back for real, and I'll tell you what happened to him for real, and why. The way I look at it, you're getting the better end of the deal."

"My momma told me not to make deals with the Devil," I heard myself say. I'd have backed away, if my legs were listening to my brain, but at that moment they weren't. So I stood there, frozen, as the Devil stalked up to me. He faced me then, nose to nose, eye to eye across that line of dead grass.

"If I wanted your soul, I'd have it a hundred ways before you knew it was missing. Drinking, lying, fornicating, pride—I've got my hooks in you so deep they're meeting in the middle. But like I said, I'm just offering you truth for truth. Neither of us gets anything but words from the other. Oh, and you," he said, pointing that long finger at me, "go first."

I thought about not answering, but that thought didn't stay long. I'd come back out there wanting answers, wanting to know what had happened to Jimmy, and why. Now here I was with the chance to learn the truth, the real truth, and I was hesitating.

Afraid.

Afraid like I'd been that night, scared enough to go home when Jimmy'd been brave enough to stay, brave enough to park his own self right in the middle of the Tramping Ground itself, and to wait for what came next.

"I came back to see if I could talk to you," I said. The words surprised me, but they tasted like they were true, so I kept going. "I wanted to know why you did what you did to Jimmy. I wanted to know why you did it. I wanted to know if it was really," I took a deep breath and looked into those unkind eyes, "you."

"That's most of it," he said thoughtfully, and sucked on his gums for a minute. "But you're missing something."

"Like what?"

He spun on his heel and walked six steps, into the dead center of the circle. Without turning around, he spoke. "What you really want to know is why I let you get away. After all, it wouldn't have been hard to make you stay, if I'd wanted."

The cold truth of that cut at my guts. "Maybe," I forced myself to say. "Or maybe I'd already seen what I thought I wanted to see, before you ripped Jimmy up."

He shook his head, all slow and sad. "Like I said, son, you came to see something, and to bear witness to what you'd seen. That's why you brought your cameras, and your fancy night vision gear, and all that good stuff that didn't help you none. You wanted truth, and you got a bellyful, and that was enough to let you walk away with your pride."

"But now," and he spun around, arms out like a showman's, "you're thinking maybe you missed something. That your friend dead Jimmy saw something you didn't afore he died, and you're wondering if it's worth seeing. Hell, you're wondering if it's worth dying yourself, just to see. Am I right?"

"You're right," I said, and he was. You don't lie to the Devil, no sir.

"Good," he said. "You're not stupid. Now let me give you your truth, and we can see where we stand."

He cleared his throat, and for a moment I thought he might be embarrassed by the whole thing. You know, the Devil telling the truth and all. But then he started talking again, and any thought of sympathy I might have had just melted away.

"In the basic, your friend's problem was that he was in my way. That's a bad place to be, son. Look around you. What do you see?"

I looked around and didn't see much. "Trees," I said. "Mud. Some trash. Grass and weeds, maybe."

He nodded. "Right. I'd call it godforsaken, but you'd think I was trying to make a joke. The point is, a man comes out here to a place like this to think. To be alone, to walk to and fro in a little patch of dirt, and up and down in it, and not be disturbed. But then along comes your friend Jimmy, and he just plain pisses me off. And you know why?"

"Why?" I asked.

He looked me in the eye, and I looked away. "Because like I said, you were here to bear witness to something bigger than yourself. You wanted a mystery. Jimmy, he wanted to be the center of things. He wanted something to happen to him, so he could go home and tell the pretty girls all about his adventure. He wanted to make this the place for his story, if'n you know what I mean. Well, hell, that ain't right. That ain't proper. That ain't going to happen, not as long as I have power in this world. And I do have power, when I choose to raise it up in me."

The Devil's voice had been rising the whole time until it was practically a shout. His cadence was one a few preachers I'd known would have killed for, a rhythm that picked you up and carried you along until it dropped you in the silence, in the weeds of the whispers.

"I don't hold with that," he said, quiet now, his voice the sound of snake's tongue going in and out. "This is my place, and it will be until the world burns. The Jimmys of the world don't get to take that away. Not now, not ever, amen."

"Amen," I caught myself whispering, and the Devil grinned.

"Very good, boy," he said, and there was a gleam in his eye I wasn't glad to see. "Do you have what you came for?"

I looked down at my feet, half to make sure my toes were outside the circle, and half just to look away from him. "Yes. I understand what happened to Jimmy now. And I'll leave you be."

"Not so fast."

I looked up. He was staring at me, still smiling. "I said, do you have what you came for."

"Like I said, I know what happened to Jimmy, and that's what I came here for. And I don't want to end up like him, so if you'll excuse me-"

"Liar."

The word hit me like a kick to the back of the knee. It's one thing when a woman calls you a liar for making up some lame-ass excuse for forgetting to call her. It's another when the one who invented lying out of whole cloth and the unformed stuff of Creation slaps it on you.

"Excuse me?"

He leaned forward, a vulture getting ready to swoop down off his perch. "I called you a liar, boy. You going to argue with me?"

I shook my head and started backing away. "I think I've done enough talking with you tonight."

"Then just listen." I froze. "You and I both know that's not the real thing you came here for. You came to see, just like you came the other night. Well, now you've seen, all right. You've seen *me*. And that's not something to be taken lightly."

"Fact is," he continued, and started walking toward me. I clung to the notion that it was all right, that he was inside the circle and I was outside, and never the twain should meet. "Fact is that you were maybe a little too eager to see something strange, don't you think?"

He stopped, maybe six inches from the edge of the circle, and put his hands up like he was leaning against an invisible wall.

"I don't think I know what you're talking about," I said. I found my legs could move again, if a little, and so I made them do that. One slide step back, and then another, and then I froze when I saw him noticing.

"I think you do," he said. "I think you're a little too curious for your own good. So I'm going to give you something, something free."

"I don't want no gifts from you, sir." The 'sir' was involuntary, and his smile got nasty when he heard it.

"It's not the sort of thing you refuse, son. The Devil wants to give you a gift, you take it. You take it and you say thank you, or he might decide to give you another one."

"I've got everything I want from you," I said.

"No, you don't," he replied, and stepped out of the circle. Grass died under his boots as he took slow steps toward me. "What, you thought there was some magic keeping me in there? You didn't draw that circle, son. Wasn't no medicine man or priest, neither. I walked that line, and I made that boundary, and I can cross it any time I please."

"Please." I echoed him. "I just want to go." My knees felt weak, felt like they were going to buckle.

The Devil shook his head, and brought his hand up in benediction. "I don't think so. You see, you gave me something tonight. It isn't often I get a chance to explain myself, and there's a certain pleasure in that. So if you gave me something, it's only right and proper that I give you something back. And if what you want is to see, well, I can give you Sight."

My legs gave out, and I dropped to my knees. "No," I said. "I don't want to see any more."

The Devil placed his hand on my forehead. "What you want is about the least important thing in the world right now. I give you Sight, so you can see what's hiding under the skin of the world. Some of it's my handiwork, some of it's the other fella's. Down these parts, you'll see a lot more that's mine. This is haunted country, son, and I give it to you in all its glory and terror. 'Cause I been working real hard, and it's about damn time someone could appreciate what I done."

Then he said something in some language I don't know and don't want to know, and his hand caught fire. And that fire, it poured down his fingers and into those sharp black nails, and from there it flowed like oily water and cheap wine into my eyes. It burned, so help me, it burned. It burned away my old way of seeing, it burned away my old eyes. I could feel it pouring in and filling every fiber, could feel it thrumming through me like a high tension wire in the wind.

And then he pulled his hand away, and I Saw.

Saw the molten hell-rock of the Tramping Ground, stamped flat with a thousand hoof prints just underneath that white dirt and sand. I saw shapes moving in the forest that weren't beasts and weren't men. I looked up and saw a line in the sky where an angel had flown by, and it was so beautiful I wanted to just sit down and cry.

"One other thing," he said, and that snapped my attention right back. There were no angels here, and none coming to help me neither.

"Yessir?" I said.

He smiled. "You've laid eyes on the Devil, and you're going to walk away after you've done so. That's a rare thing, son, a rare and powerful thing. But that also means you've had the Devil's eyes upon you, and once I've seen you, up close and personal like this, I don't ever stop seeing you. I'll know where you are, boy. I'll know where to find you. You'll have the Devil looking over your shoulder any time I damn well please to cast my eye that way, and you'll be thinking 'bout that every time you kiss your mother's cheek or make love to that long-legged whore you call a lady friend. That's where the real price for your answer starts to be paid, boy. As for the rest of it? I'll think of other things. I always do."

I swallowed hard. "I don't know what I could ever do for you, sir."

"You will," he said. "Now go. I got some thinking to do." And he turned and started walking away, and where he did the hell-rock bubbled up around his feet.

I waited 'til I was sure he couldn't see me, and then I turned and ran back down to the road. Nothing followed me but his laughter, but that was enough.

# AFTERPARTY:
# — or, NOT OUT OF THE WOODS —
## Chaz Brenchley

*The enchanted forest is found in fairytales around the world. In real life, woods look mysterious and they are full of both danger and opportunity. The woods are homes for a myriad of organisms, some of which are poisonous, some of which are predators, and some of which are food. Night falls sooner in the woods than anywhere else, and even in mid-day it's hard to see between the trees. A deer can escape from a hunter in the woods with ease, and a bear can take the hunter completely by surprise. Is it so strange to picture that unicorns could hide between the trees, or that bears can talk? In folklore, enchanted forests are places of magic, adventure, and transformation.*

*Enchanted forests can be places of menace or refuge, hindrance or help. Sometimes they are all of these things, in turn. The Beast's castle in "Beauty and the Beast" is located in the forest, and at various points in the story it is a place of menace, redemption, and physical and spiritual transformation. Hansel and Gretel find an evil witch's' cottage in the forest, and Snow White finds refuge in the cottage of the dwarves. In many fairy tales and in medieval romances, the woods are a place to find love, often in surprising ways. For instance, a different Snow White, the sister of Rose Red, marries a prince who was transformed into a bear, while Rose Red marries the prince's brother.*

*Enchanted forest stories can take many forms, but they carry common threads of mystery, magic, and transformation. The protagonist of an enchanted forest story enters the woods (or lives in the woods and encounters something new about them) and has an adventure, after which they are not the same. Sometimes the story is inverted—instead of the hero coming to the woods, the woods come to the hero. A bear stumbles into the sisters' cottage and becomes a prince. An imp who lives in the woods appears before an imprisoned girl and helps her turn straw into gold. The theme of mystery and transformation holds true. The woods give you what you need, if not want you want.*

———◄●►———

I t's not a wake, though, right?"

"It's not a wake, Gordy, no. We *had* a wake. Remember?"

"'Course I remember, I was there."

"Too right you were. Which is why I doubt you can remember."

"I remember you. Stepping politely outside to throw up in the gutter, like you were still a kid."

"Honey, you obviously didn't know me as a kid. I was never that polite. I'd throw up on anything. Anyone. Quin knew."

"I'm sure."

"Hell, it was Quin's fault, more often than not. He had no sense of rationing the young—"

"Enough, people. Seriously. We need to decide if we're doing this or not. It's not a wake; it's not for Quin at all. This one's for Gerard. Look, we had this amazing year, yeah? We were amazing. We'll never be that good again. We gave Quin his long farewell, we took care of him all the way; we saw him out and we buried him and we drank a tot or two, or in Gordy's case a bottle. And through it all Gerard was in the house, living it; and I guess we did what we could for him but it wasn't about him, it couldn't be. And it strikes me now that I never saw him crack a smile, even when the rest of us were romping. He carried all of us, if you ask me, more than any of us knew, and he shouldn't have had to do that. And now he's doing the hardest thing, he's selling up and moving on, moving out; and if we let him he'll pack and sort that whole bloody house by himself, and I just don't think he should have to do that. Many hands make light work; we could do it for him in a weekend."

"We could, aye. And we'll get under his feet and in his way like we always did, going way back, before Quin was even sick. And he'll scowl behind his glasses and flay us with that awful masterful sarcastic voice of his, and you think he'll *enjoy* that? You think he'll be *grateful*?"

"Yes, I do. More than that, I think he needs it. I don't think he actually can do this by himself, I think it'll break him. The house always needed the two of them to keep it in check. With Quin gone... Well. That's why he's selling, of course. He should have done it sooner. But what say, people? Are we doing this?"

"Hell, yes."

"Of course we are."

"Did you even need to ask?"

———◖●◗———

It's not the house. It never was the house. I didn't say a word because I didn't need to, they took me for granted as they always had, as they always should have done—but I could have told them better, if I ever thought they'd listen. Not the house.

The house is a 'twenties suburban semi, on a lane that overlooks a park and then peters out into woodland, one of those urban pockets of an older England entirely subsumed by an overreaching population that doesn't know, that never will know what jewels it has swallowed down.

At least the trees survive, that odd little isolated patch of them: something to be grateful for. There's enough wood there for kids to scare themselves, for teenagers to hang out and hide up, for older men—us—to take a walk, take a break when things got too much with Quin and the park below was just too open and exposed. Trauma nurtures the furtive in all of us; at one time or another we all need to run for cover.

The park's Victorian, and untouchable. Even the railings are original. They run along the south side of the lane; the north side is built up all the way, fifty houses just like Quin's, tucked side by side and here's hoping you get on with your neighbours.

I asked him once, why that house, why there? He smiled and said, "For the boys, of course. They come out of the trees, ready for anything; someone needs to be here, to pick them up." He gave me a moment to think about that, and then he said, "As I remember, you were one of them, weren't you, Jody?"

I gave him a smile for remembering and a kiss for my name, because this was quite late in the year, and by then he wasn't always sure quite who we were or where our stories crossed. I said, "Oh, I surely was. And I've been here or hereabouts ever since, and I'm not sure I ever said thank you. Not properly."

"Of course not. You'd never let me down that badly. I trained you better."

His voice was as thin as his bones by then, and that was as much talk as he was good for, he who used to run on and on at the mouth as though he had words banked up, reservoirs and oceans, as though he never could run dry.

I slipped a cube of cold beef consommé between his lips, and left him to suck on it. Which he would do because it was soothing to his throat and strong to his palate, something he could taste yet, something to absorb him; which we wanted him to do because it was pure protein almost, the better part of a cow boiled down, something to absorb.

I should know, I'd made it. When I wasn't sitting with him, I spent most of my time in the kitchen—but there was nothing new in that. I always had.

As I came walking down the lane, early that Saturday morning, there were half a dozen more of us sitting on the garden wall, all in a line. We never used to show up so many altogether, we had a roster and we stuck to it, pretty much; but Quin's last days changed that, and the days after. We were all there for his leaving, for the funeral and the wake—and then we made a mess of it afterwards, because you can draw up a roster for nursing a sick friend but not for visiting his bereaved. Especially not when it's Gerard. He'd have known. So we turned up in awkward clumps, or else not at all for days on end; and when he grew tired of that he just locked up the house and went away for a while.

Once he was back we did plan, we phoned around in the old round robin and agreed to leave him strictly alone until he invited us. Which he did, by twos and threes, for dinner or a concert or a gallery opening, all those things we couldn't do with Quin. And we went, of course; and we gave him invitations in our turn, militarily, by ones and twos in strict rotation; and almost everything was edgy and we almost never saw each other except like that, in small parties with Gerard.

Until he let Pete know that he was moving, and Pete called us all to the pub; and now we were here, and now this, one last gathering of the clan.

"You did let him know, right, Pete? That we were coming to help?"

"Of course I did; he's expecting a crowd. And a skip. I thought maybe we'd wait out here until the skip turns the corner, so we can overwhelm him in a very helpful rush. Did you bring breakfast, in that attractive basket?"

"You know I did. Fresh croissants and lemon marmalade for now, but I guess we'll be working hard; there's a slab of bacon and a couple of dozen eggs for second breakfast." And a pair of sourdough loaves that I didn't need to mention, and what more I had scavenged from the larder to keep people going. I'd have to shop for lunch, but everyone knew that; they'd all pitch in. And for the inevitable alcohol, we wouldn't raid Gerard's cellar—or rather we would, but not without contributing.

"Here comes the skip. Bang on nine, as promised. Guys, you go round the back, let yourselves in. Tell him I'm dealing with the skip guy, and he won't even need to move his car. Jody—"

"Straight into the kitchen, coffee and croissants, keep him sweet. I know."

You'll always find me in the kitchen at parties. It's Quin's fault, more or less. Mostly more. He taught me to cook; more, he laid it out for me that it was actually an option, that rough ragged boys could learn the skill of it, the art and the craft together. Which started with eating, learning how to eat. The first meal he ever made me, pork and mushrooms flambéed in brandy, sauced with cream, green beans in butter on the side: I had no idea it was even possible, let alone that it might be so easy. Bread and a fork and a bottle of Sancerre, I was in pig heaven. I was seventeen, what did I know? He pitched it perfectly; that was his gift. Another boy he might have charmed with music, or with books. The house was full of both. I guess any seventeen-year-old can eat, but Quin knew to push me further.

He always did know, what boy in which direction. And there were always boys passing through for him to exercise that talent on, before me and after me, just the same. He found us, or we him: he helped us grow and let us go, and when we checked back there were already others, newly in place. In our places. It almost, almost didn't matter.

We were the generation that reclaimed him at the end, though. He was ours, we were his; we got to keep him. A bunch of middle-aged men, seeing one of their own through to his long home. He had fifteen years on me, no more. At seventeen, that had seemed an age. It had been an age. At forty? Not so much.

Not all of us had come to him as boys. There were students and graduate students, one or two of us were faculty or friends from otherwhere—and of course there was Gerard, who was something else altogether. Still: we were all of an age now, regardless of when we'd met him. All within a decade of each other, with all that that implied. Which was largely possessiveness and cohesion, mixed: of course we'd kept him to ourselves, through that long last year when he wouldn't go back into hospital. Of course we coped, of course we bonded. Some of us hadn't been friends before this all began; some of us still weren't, and never would be. Nevertheless. We were here and doing this, one last effort for the group, for the thing that we had been.

*A brotherhood of blood*, we called it, but it was more than that. Brighter, sharper. A brotherhood of blades, who shed blood only incidentally.

Gerard was grumpy as ever, first thing. I fed him caffeine and carbs while I let him see how organised we were, how on top of what needed done. There was the skip in the driveway, for everything we chucked; here came the shredders, for whatever papers he didn't need to keep; here were the boxes, to take the books and CDs that he did. Sit down and watch, and try a *pain au chocolat*. There's nothing else to do.

Of course that wasn't true, it couldn't be. This was his house. We only called it Quin's from courtesy and long habit and that sense of occupation that has naught to do with deeds and mortgages. Here he held court; here he brought us, fed us, revealed us to ourselves. He was gone now, but even so. More than memories remained. Those were Quin's books that lined each room from floor to ceiling, Quin's papers that overflowed the filing cabinets: one last heedless gift, a weight shrugged off for someone else to deal with. On paper, that was Gerard. In practice we meant it to be us, but we couldn't actually make the core decisions. What to pitch and what to pack, what to donate, what to recycle: Gerard had at least to lay down ground rules, so that we could filter out the easy choices before we took edge cases in to him.

Even to me, even in the kitchen, that applied. I was packing as I cooked: stripping shelves, filling boxes, leaving cupboards empty in my wake. Gerard was handy in the kitchen; of course he'd want the good knives, the seasoned wok, the Le Creuset and the Microplanes. The slow-cooker, though, we'd bought that in to make the stocks I simmered down for Quin's constant consommé—would he want to keep that with him, or should I take it home? What about the spice rack Quin had improvised from a wardrobe shoe hanger—and what about the spices? Half of them were faded dusty ghosts, liable only to fade further. The more I dug about, the more I had to check with Gerard. And every time there was someone else ahead of me, checking whether he wanted something else, the SF paperbacks or the hand-labelled cassette tapes or an envelope of photos or a lamp.

Gerard had settled in his own study, surrounded by his own unequi-vocal things. He exuded patience and tolerance and reason, and reminded me of nothing so much as a ticking bomb. Gin was safe to defuse him, but not at eleven in the morning—so I did the other thing, and removed myself from ground zero. Sooner than I'd planned to, I went out into the lane, with my mind on the shops around the corner.

I was waylaid, though, and not for the first time in that house. Here was Mal sitting on the wall alone, with a bottle of beer and a tight singleskin the way he liked to roll them. Of course I hitched myself up beside him, of course I took a swig from the bottle and a puff from the joint. It was something we had that not even Quin had taught us. That made it something to hold on to, that wouldn't turn slithery beneath our grasp.

Without looking in their direction, without so much as nodding his head thataway, Mal murmured, "Have you noticed, over the road there...?"

"Oh, yeah." Inside the park railings, in the shadow of a great oak, two lads were watching us. Middle-aged men in their territory, passing beer and a smoke back and forth—of course they were watching.

"Remind you of anyone?"

"Hell, no. We were never that thin."

"Yeah, we were. We were exactly that thin. And that nosy." And Quin wasn't here now to beckon them in, and you couldn't really call it a decision, but Mal and I were both suddenly on our feet and strolling over.

"Hey." They gazed at us through the railings, wary, curious, a little confused. Mal made things easier by taking out his wallet. "You lads fancy picking up some cash?"

Of course they did. One of them was quicker to ask, "What for?"

"A day of your time and a bit of heavy lifting, that's all. We're clearing out the house, and we're all three times your age and only half as flexible. Twenty up front, we'll feed you and beer you up and give you another twenty when we're done. That sound okay?"

"Each?"

"Of course, each. And the same again tomorrow if you can come back. Just if you're up for it, no pressure."

They were so up for it, the gate at the corner was too far away. One of them swarmed the railings and was holding out his hand before his mate was halfway over.

The nice thing was, he wasn't reaching for Mal's cash. Not yet. He was introducing himself, and his friend: "I'm Jonah. The slow one's Ben."

"Fuck you, Jonah," came down a little breathlessly from where the other boy was perched in discomfort atop the railings. Jonah's thin cool hand in mine and a tentative grip, playing grown-up with strangers, and then the necessary light relief behind him, "Oh, *fuck it*," as Ben jumped down with his jeans snagged on a spike and we could all hear the seam tearing.

Jonah sniggered as boys will, as no doubt he would again and again as he made a story of it, as he told it again and again. Mal was instantly practical: "Not to worry, we've got needle and thread in the house. And half a dozen men who can sew, if you can't; and other jeans you can borrow in the meantime. Hell, we've got other jeans you can keep, if you find a pair you like. That's the point of this, we're getting rid of stuff. We all used to keep a change of clothes here, and most of them are still cluttering up the spare room…"

I let him lead them away while I just stood in the roadway there, watching; and none of that was about seeing how badly Ben had ripped the seat out of his jeans, or hoping for a lewd glimpse of his boxers. I was timetripping again, watching us follow Quin inside, twenty years ago. More. Hearing his voice again, *they come out of the trees, ready for anything.*

Hoping these lads were up for it; and trailing in behind them to find out, just when I had expected to go shopping.

Bashful Ben, freshly denim'd in nearly-new black CKs that I already figured we were never getting back, found his voice at last in the front room that had been Quin's at the end. Staring at the great hospital bed that stood so inherently out of place among the books and the albums and the faded silk brocade, he said, "What's the story here, then?"

True stories take a lifetime in the making, in the telling, in the fact of them. These boys would have their own, that we'd pick up in echoes and missed beats and hesitancies, the mouse-overs of conversation; they wouldn't know yet how to listen for those in us. I brought them beers, while Mal gave them something so raw and abbreviated it was almost untrue, it said so little. "Gerard—the big man in the back study—used to share this house with his partner. But Quin was sick, and he was a long time dying, and a bunch of us nursed him here at home. The bed's going to a charity now. That's something you could do for us, actually; it needs taking apart and carrying outside, they're coming to pick it up this afternoon. Come on, I'll show you where the spanners are…"

Boys and tools and beer, noise and work and tubular steel; nothing could be more right. We left them to it. I borrowed Gordy and his car for the run to the shops, figuring that we were going to need more of everything. More than I could carry, more than we could possibly imagine, just altogether more.

By the time we came back, Quin's bed was a neatly stacked pile of puzzle-pieces leant against the skip, and the boys were less neatly leaning on that same convenient prop, sharing a cigarette and a quiet chat. I grinned, warned them not to smoke in the house, and enrolled them to shift the contents of Gordy's car into the kitchen. "Beer in the fridge, wine on the counter, food on the table. Is either of you any good at building sandwiches? No, that's what I figured. When we're done unloading, check with Pete, but I think everything that's left in the garage can go straight into the skip..."

People ate on the fly; I was as busy as anyone, keeping up. There were runs to charity shops, runs to the secondhand bookshop. The disassembled bed went away. Filing cabinets replaced it, lined up orderly in the driveway and supposedly for sale. Jonah thought his mum might like one; everyone knew it was hers for the asking.

And nothing about the day was easy, but the boys did make it easier. Like oil in the workings, slippery and alien and getting everywhere. And they might have been us, they must have been us, we must have been just like that. Lean and intrusive and flexible as ferrets, brash and expectant like awkward, eager dogs. Jonah talked all the time, Ben never spoke from choice: it didn't matter. They were still interchangeable, interchangeably me, interchangeably us.

More and more I felt it, as the house emptied around us. Quin's stuff went away, and I'd thought that would reveal more and more of Quin; I'd looked to see the real man exposed, in the absence of his trappings. I'd thought we'd be haunted by memories, talking all day just to keep the loss at bay, sharing old stories and old photographs and wrapping grief about us like a blanket against the brute blunt impact of bared shelves, bared floors, bared hearts.

It didn't happen. Something was happening, though, something else. The boys were shifting furniture overhead, ripping up ancient carpets, lugging them out to the skip. Everything about that was loud: coarse laughter and clumping feet, heave and drag and a sudden resounding yell when the foot of a dresser came down unexpectedly on the foot of a startled adolescent.

"The house sounds wrong," Pete murmured, reaching for a pasty.

"No, it doesn't. It just hasn't sounded this way for a while," hollow and busy both at once. It wasn't the nostalgia I'd expected, but I remembered this. When we built the bookshelves all through the house, room by room; or that summer we chased Quin and Gerard off to Greece and decorated everywhere, new wallpaper, fresh paint; and then ten years later when we did the same again, when they were away in China. Hell, more recently than that, when we shifted everything around to make the front room over to Quin in his entirety, all contained within that one small space. It had taken work to fit him in on that mechanical insect of a bed with his familiar organic comforts around him, his furniture and curtains, his texts, his friends.

Now we were doing the other thing, unpicking Quin from the fabric of the house, which was the fabric of our lives. It should have been momentous. It could have been unbearable. Even Gerard was dealing, though, better than anyone might have anticipated. His glasses flashed blankly threatening from time to time, but if it never got worse than that, we'd have a better day than ever we had hoped for.

Actually I thought we were having a bigger day than any of us imagined. I felt as though we were in the grip of something greater than ourselves, and perhaps we always had been: a narrative unfolding, weighty and irresistible, like a bolt of cloth flung across the landscape. I thought we were possessed, reclaimed, appropriated.

It wasn't, it couldn't be about the house. We were leaving the house, disassembling it. Taking that whole artefact apart. We'd build again, but otherwise: different relationships in different places, not this. *We'll never be that good again*—Pete had said it, and it was true, and we did all feel it.

It wasn't, it couldn't be about Quin, either. I'd always thought we lived in his story, but apparently not. *Someone needs to be here, to pick them up*. Maybe he really meant that, as though he was as interchangeable as the rest of us, playing out a role as written, occupying a space already defined for him. He liked to claim that boys came out of the wood fully formed, newly sprung, seeking the lives they were meant to inhabit. Families and histories, school reports and medical records were just the universe giving them a hasty retcon, a necessary backstory. I used to tell him that was the ultimate in solipsism, the narcissist in him running rampant; that Mal and I had absolutely existed BQ, before he met us just up the lane there, in the shadow of the trees, his prime exemplar. He said of course we'd believe that, it was crucial to the fiction that we buy into it. You can't doubt your own legend.

By that logic, Jonah never had a mother until he needed one, until he said she'd like a filing cabinet. Then there was a shift in creation, a rearrangement, and there she was: just half a mile distant and they'd lived there all his life. No point trying to call her, he said, she never charged her phone. He'd just trot down there to confirm. He'd be back for supper.

Of course he would. No boy ever missed a home-cooked curry. I called the stranded Ben into the kitchen, to save him having to talk with any of the others or, horror of horrors, Gerard himself. We had the big man mellowing on gin, but he'd spent all day shredding Quin's most personal documents, which of course meant rereading half the story of his life, while the rest of us dismantled his home around him. I wouldn't push a kid under that particular bus, no matter how mellow. This particular kid had gone in to empty the shredders a time or two; I thought that was exposure enough.

So I kept him with me, showed him how to chop an onion, let him look over my shoulder while I mixed spices and fried chicken, simmered lentils, boiled rice. Ordinarily I don't like anyone else in my kitchen, but the day wasn't ordinary and the kitchen wasn't mine, and an apprentice has his uses even where he slows you down. There's a pleasure in passing on skills, sharing knowledge; maybe it's even a duty. And it might be the last time in this house. I could call it a salute, a gesture of gratitude, an old debt settled. I am not Quin—I had to keep reminding myself of that, *I am not Quin*—but I could learn to be. I had to keep ignoring the little voice that said so, *I could learn to be.* Quin had forged a thing and left it with us, left us with it. Not the house.

We still had the bulk of the furniture, at least one more day, so we could eat around the Georgian dining-table that last time. All the linens were packed away; Ben and I set china out on bare unthinkable wood, and passed inconceivable kitchen-roll for napkins. Gerard's expression was a masterpiece.

He plied knife and fork judgmentally, but we'd made a mound of chapattis, Ben and I, so most of us ate with our fingers. It was an art new to the boys, and of course they made a mess of it, all over the precious walnut; but the table had suffered much this last year and was already headed for the French polishers before it went to Gerard's new place, so even he only shrugged and said "Wipe it up."

After dinner, young Jonah coopted Gordy to wrestle one of the filing cabinets into the back of his car and deliver it and Jonah home. They both seemed to assume that Ben would be going with them—especially once Jonah had made mention of the two flights of stairs at the other end, up to his mother's flat—but I put the kibosh on that.

"House rule," I said. "Whoever cooks does the dishes too. That's me and Ben, tonight. And the dishwasher's gone, so..."

So I got to keep him an hour longer, because house rules are inflexible, even in the last days of the house. I told him, when he grumbled: "It's not about the house. It's not about the rules either, in any inflexible sense. It's certainly not about justice. It's about choice and community, and not making work for other people. Sometimes a whole meal goes together in a single pot; sometimes you use every pan in the place, like we did tonight. We chose to do that," or I did, which came to the same thing, "so this was our choice too," the vast array of dirty dishes stacked on every surface in the kitchen. "Which means we get to deal with it, and leave things lovely for whoever makes breakfast in the morning." Chances were, that would be me too, with or without my new assistant. I didn't say so. If he wanted to be here early tomorrow—or at all—it had to come from him. Boys step out of the trees; we don't call them forth. It's another house rule, immutable. Still nothing to do with the house. It wasn't about to change, just because the house went away.

Conversely, though, it was perfectly fine to lead them back into the trees. When we were done, the last plate stacked and the last pan boxed up—no grand dinner tomorrow, we'd be eating takeaway on our knees, or else going out somewhere local and easy—I said, "Okay, that's that. Thanks for all your help today, Ben, you've been a star. Now you want a smoke, and I want a walk. Come with me?"

"'Course, yeah."

Ten minutes later we were deep in the wood, our solemn progress interrupted by muttered teenage curse-words as Ben caught his new jeans on brambles and stumbled over rocks and dips in the path until I wondered just how much he'd been drinking through the day. Or smoking. Maybe that was fitting, because for sure Quin had never rationed us when we were kids. *I am not Quin,* but even so. I didn't mind sending him home happy

Or maybe he was just being sixteen, nothing to do with beer or pot. God knew, I'd been clumsy enough at that age; and it was too dark to watch his awkward adolescent feet, too dark to see anything much until blind memory brought me into a clearing at the heart of the wood.

Here was a felled trunk we could sit on, under the cold stars. There was the flare of his cigarette as he inhaled. Just tobacco, I thought, probably.

"So," I said. "Good day?"

"Awesome," he said. Well-fed and well-satisfied and forty quid richer, that was enough for him. He probably hadn't learned to value the ache in his muscles and the merits of working with other people for someone else's good—but perhaps I was too cynical, because he went on, "It's a bit sad, though, innit?"

"Is it? Why's that, what's sad?"

"Us finding you now, just when you're all going. That house must've been awesome, and it's been there all this time, and we never knew."

"Quin was fairly special," I agreed, though he would have said that any nostalgia for time lost was an artefact, that Ben had no past until he'd found it necessary to invent one.

"Not him. I mean, not just him. All of you. The whole house, all those books and things. That kitchen."

He'd been well impressed by all the spices. But *it's not about the house*, and now at last I could say that aloud. "It's not about the house. That's just bricks and things. World's full of bricks and things." World was full of boys too, but I didn't tell him that. I didn't need to. Every boy knows how very transitory he is. Woven of moonlight in the trees' shadow, there's always another coming. Something in the wood compels them, unless it's something in our lives, a need, an absence, a blank space ready to be filled.

"Not my world," he said. "That place was special, and it's gone." *We only found it in time to tear it down,* he was saying.

"What you found was us," I said stubbornly. "Not the house. The house was already in splinters," and the splinters were in our hearts. "Each of us, where we go, we take something of that with us. And none of us is going far. It was Gerard's home, not ours; he's moving the other side of town, but most of us are closer. I'm ten minutes' walk from here. The house gave us a focus, sure, but we'll find another," or else we'd fly apart, without Quin to bind us all together. I might have been expecting that, but suddenly I wasn't sure any more. "Maybe it wasn't the house at all." *Or Quin.* "This place, here in the woods, we all used to come here all the time." *We came from here, some of us, if you want to listen to Quin. This is where boys happen.*

"This wood is like the bones of old England, jutting up—but the thing about bones, they run under the skin, further than you know. There's not much left of it now, but it used to be much larger. That park, where we found you? That tree, that big oak we found you under? That used to be part of this, before the Victorians tidied every-thing up and put a fence around the pretty bit. So did the lane, so did everything round about here. That house was built on the memory of trees. We came out of the woods: you did, we did. We found each other. It used to be Quin who found us, but he wasn't ever the start of it, and he isn't the end of it either. It's a cycle, a relay race, something. Something gets passed on."

He was busy lighting one cigarette from the butt of another, so he didn't say anything. Maybe he wouldn't have said anything anyway. But he stared out past the glow, through the smoke, into the dark heart of the wood; and maybe there was a splinter there too, and always had been.

# — THE SLECK —
## Keris McDonald

*Every suburb has a place that resists being tamed—a muddy patch of creek,
a corner of the park that's always overgrown and shadowy, a culvert large
enough to play in and small enough to be scary, an abandoned house. These
places are parent repellent and kid magnets. Parents see these places and
realize that the muddy creek is just deep enough to drown a child. That
overgrown patch of park is the perfect place to hide a body. That culvert could
flood, or be full of rats, or harbor tetanus. Kids see these places and see a place
where no parents will watch them, and where they can have an adventure.
The more parents warn their kids away from the suspect places, the faster
kids run to them.*

*These patches of wildness usually don't show up on registries of haunted
places, but suburb kids can you tell you all about them. They know that the
creek behind the school that parents fear is a safe haven, but the parking lot
behind the donut shop is not. They know that you can hear whispers if you
stand outside the house where the lady who collected all the parakeets died
last year. They know the whole secret life of the suburbs, where their parents
see only the surface.*

*Suburb parents get a lot of things wrong but there's one thing they are
right about. Kids may be great at seeing the secret life of the world, but they
aren't very good about telling the difference between friends and enemies. The
suburbs are full of shape-shifters and lurking monsters. That boy who seems
so charming is really a wolf. That girl who says she's your friend is really a
witch. Sure, the kids think the creek is a safe haven, but that's because the
creek is clever. The creek and the meadow and the culvert and the old house
are traps that can spring in an instant. "The Sleck", by Keris MacDonald,
is a terrifying and heartbreaking tale of what happens when those traps are
sprung.*

**B**etween two of the eight-foot concrete posts, a corner of the
chain-link fence had been pulled up to make a gap. Rob could
see a crumpled and rusty bicycle lying beyond, choked by the
rough grass.

Kids, he guessed. It was impossible to keep them out.

"You idiots," he growled, leaning against his car where it was parked up at the curb. It had only been a year, for chrissakes. A year exactly, today. "You stupid wee idiots. You've got no fucking sense, have you?"

If he'd been sober he would have left it at that. He'd only come to look, after all—to look at the fence and leave the bunch of flowers he'd bought at the petrol station from the Sikh woman who'd wrinkled her nose at the smell of beer on his breath.

But he wasn't sober. It was a year today since Bethany had gone off to play with her friends in the Sleck. And Rob had been drinking since breakfast, just as June had been crying since she woke up. Slow and steady, like.

Not that he was drunk drunk. He'd driven here without incident, after all. He might not be entirely sober, but he'd reached a state of myopic clarity. Everything in front of him—the fence, the downhill slope of grass, the scrubby willow trees lifting their yellowing leaves to the sun—seemed in perfect focus. Everything beyond—the sprawling housing-estate that spread in every direction—was blurred and irrelevant.

Only the Sleck was real.

The fucking Sleck.

He remembered playing down there himself, as a kid. There's been fewer houses around then, of course. This road where he was standing had been allotment gardens instead. But the neighboring estates had grown together over the years—seventies' red bricks giving way to modern yellow ones, and big gardens where men used to grow potatoes and leeks to feed the children now built over with tiny starter homes for the modern family unit. Yet they'd never built over the Sleck, a teardrop-shaped patch of wilderness in a valley now trapped by the rising tide of development. Shallow at the narrow end, sloping down to a deep dell that was a swamp in summer and a pond in winter—maybe it was an old mine-working, some long-collapsed and overgrown shaft from the coal-fields hereabouts. It certainly had the look of a sinkhole. Even in his day, before the invention of Health and Safety, or parents giving a shit where the bairns were off to, it had had a dire reputation.

What was it they'd said...? Rob, in his beer-fug, couldn't quite recall. Yet now as then, it was a magnet for local children, though it was fenced off and strictly forbidden.

Today all seemed quiet. The September school term had just started. If there were any skivers drinking cider and smoking weed down there, they were well-hidden amongst the trees. The only noise that came to Rob's ears was from the occasional passing cars at his back.

If he'd been sober he would have sat in his own vehicle and let the tears fall.

Fuck it.

Crouching right down, he ducked under the triangular flap of loose fencing, and through. The grass on the far side was uncut, knee-deep and studded with tall thistles, but a narrow path had been worn through the yellowing stalks and led away downhill. Brown speckled moths fluttered up around him as he took his first steps. He glanced behind him once at his car, which looked oddly forlorn on the roadside there.

He could remember the scene a year ago—the fence pulled down, ambulance tracks gouged through the grass, and blue flashing police lights stabbing the yellow evening. And the crowd lined up along the pavement. Staring.

They'd done their best, the neighbours. They'd turned out in their dozens to look for Bethany when June had become frantic with worry that afternoon. They'd cut through the fencing to let the medics in closer. They'd closed ranks and turned their backs on Elliot and Imogen's families, expressing their disapproval. Imogen's family had even moved away to another estate, unable to bear the blame heaped on their daughter.

Rob and June had moved house too. Not out of guilt, but because they couldn't stand walking past and seeing where it had happened.

Where they'd found her.

Down here.

The path took him down the long slope at a diagonal. Nearest the road there was a lot of the usual litter and detritus dumped in the grass, but the further down the hillside he descended, the more the rubbish thinned out and the longer grew the grass in which the narrow paths wound and criss-crossed. It stood elbow-tall soon, the dry seed-heads scattering their pale ticks on Rob's clothes, goose-grass and fat burrs clinging to his shoelaces and cuffs like an infestation of vermin. He reached the first of the scrubby sallows just as the incline flattened out. Lengths of plank propped loosely in the branches suggested that someone had had the idea of building a tree-house, but had not known where to take the plan. Ahead of him the trees grew thicker, and tall sedges with their feathery rust-colored heads showed in the gaps beyond. Bright spots of yellow announced the last flowers of the yellow flag-irises.

Rob swatted away the flies that were circling his head. Now that he had dropped below the surrounding skyline there was no breeze. He could smell the damp too; that compost-heap aroma of mulching leaves. There was the beginning of something that looked like a crude boardwalk, mismatched planks laid end-to-end forming a trail that led into the trees. He moved toward it, hearing the slight squelch of moisture under his feet. The burned carcass of a motorbike marked the start of the trail. It was buried up to its engine in the earth, and thistles were growing up through the rusty skeleton.

It hadn't taken the youths long to reclaim their territory, Rob thought sourly.

He stepped onto the first plank and walked slowly out along its length, noting the way the spongy wood sagged. The first tree he reached had no single central trunk but instead a mass of stems, most of which seemed not to have the energy to lift themselves from the ground; the biggest branches sprawled horizontally before rising skyward, and to reach the walkway that continued on the far side he found he had to climb through the tangle of trunks and twigs. The bark was rough under his hands.

I'm too big, he thought dizzily, forcing a path because he couldn't focus far enough ahead to plan a route. Twigs snapped. Discarded plastic bottles winked up at him from the weeds like translucent toads. Dirt from the shaken leaves sifted down on the back of his head and slid down his collar. He scratched at his neck, feeling lodes of dust gather under his nails. His woollen donkey-jacket was too hot, and he angrily fought off the branches that smacked his face.

After three more trees the beer was running out of him with his sweat and his left foot was wet where he'd slid off a branch and squelched into black earth that smelled of old eggs. But he stepped down onto the last plank, feeling it sag and suck beneath him, then out into full daylight. This was as far as the trail went, ending in a wooden industrial pallet resting on a crust of algaed mud. Beyond that stood a patch of reed-mace or bulrushes or whatever they were, shoulder high and growing straight out of the water.

Rob shuddered, the breath coming out of his lungs in a rasp. What the hell were those stupid kids thinking of? Getting the pallet here must have taken huge effort. Was it supposed to be a raft or a jetty or what? Did they come down here to fish in the shallow water?

Jesus, what did they think they could catch?

He stepped gingerly onto the wooden slats and looked down over the far edge into the water. That lying surface reflected only the sky, as if it were equally infinite in depth.

The pool had been six inches deep when they found Bethany face-down in it. Only six inches, so she should have been able to stand up, but under the water there was no solid bottom, just a thick sucking mud that it was impossible to push against.

He thought about her little hands, pushing down frantically into the muck. Trying to raise her face above the surface.

She'd only ever swum in inflatable armbands.

"Oh Christ," he said, sagging with pain.

There was one last tin of Fosters stowed in the pocket of his jacket. He pulled out the can and cracked the ring-pull, grateful for the little hiss that was the only promise of comfort. Swigging from the can, he washed the beer around in his mouth, trying to dispel the sulfurous smell of the black ooze that rose from the beneath the beached pallet. Then he hunkered down on his heels. There was a Coke tin crushed and wedged in between two of the slats at his feet. He prodded it with one finger as he sniffed back his pain, craving distraction, but it did not shift. He sucked his dry lips and looked around him blearily. The loss of a little height had changed the view completely. The vegetation hid all sight of the surrounding houses and all but a patch of sky, surrounding him with a wall of greens and browns. He could have been in the middle of some marsh a hundred miles across, for all he could tell. Some primitive swamp crawling with druids and boar and woad-painted savages.

Flies whined about his head.

Setting the tin down on the wood, he reached into his jacket again, the inside of it this time—the so-called poacher's pocket. Tucked away against his ribs were two small objects, and he drew them out now and held them reverently before him.

A teddy bear. A soft-bodied doll with ginger woolen hair and purple-striped leggings. Mr. Paws and Chloe, Bethany had named them. Chloe's skinny cloth legs dangled limply from under her dress. Like a drowning victim.

Roy had clung to Bethany's stretcher and kept pace as the paramedics carried it up the hill, but they all knew already that it was too late. "Why can't they keep their kids out of this place?" he'd heard one constable mutter to another. The question hadn't been meant to be overheard. Or answered.

There were a lot of questions like that.

Why didn't we find her in time?

What did we do to deserve this?

They had retraced Bethany's movements at last, after they finally found Imogen and Elliot cowering and sullen in their respective homes, hiding from attention. The children admitted under duress that yes, she'd gone with them and some others to the Sleck. She'd gone into the water. They'd run away.

Why didn't you tell someone? June had screamed. Why didn't you get help?

There was no clear answer to that. The children's accounts were confused, and it wasn't even clear how many others had been present. Their story kept shifting: Bethany had slipped, she had tried to go paddling, she'd been pushed by someone else in the group. Elliot's first version was that some 'black lady' had pulled her in, but the police discounted that as fantasy. There were no prosecutions. The children were too young to bear any sort of witness.

It had been, on balance, probably an accident.

No one's fault.

But Rob had blamed Imogen. A stout and bossy nine-year-old, there was nothing attractive about her but she always had a posse of younger children in thrall. Including Bethany, who'd followed her all over the estate.

Rob could certainly imagine Imogen pushing Bethany. The mental picture had kept him awake many nights. He'd entertained terrible fantasies about what he'd have done to the nine-year-old if he'd somehow caught her in the act. Unforgiveable things that he would never voice. Not even to June.

What was the point anyway? Bethany had been buried. Imogen's family had packed up and relocated. The fence around the Sleck had been repaired and the local council had started on a long process of arguing about what to do with the place and how best to make it safe.

Rob laid Mr Paws and Chloe gently on the planks. "My bonny lass," he said softly, as tears ran down the harsh grooves the year had carved into his face, and slipped off the end of his nose. One landed on Mr Paws' worn fur. "My sweet bairn. Why'd they do it you?"

A ripple ran across the water's surface, lapping against the edge of the pallet. The surface of the water heaved like a silver skin, and then broke. Something was rising out of the mire. It moved with the slickness of crude oil and was as black as oil too, its head and shoulders rearing from the weedy slime as if it had been lying face down. The smell of the stagnant water rolled over Rob.

Blinking, he tried to focus. Tried to understand. The newcomer was female; he could see the shape of neat little breasts on its torso and he thought that under the thick coating of mud she was naked, but he could not be sure. Her hair was like ropes of pitch. Eyes opened in that glistening head and they were pondweed-green, all the more startling in that jet-black oozy face. But he wasn't surprised, or frightened. Alcohol buffered the gap between what he knew was possible, and what it was he was seeing.

"Why?" he asked her. "Why did you take her?"

She was now standing clear of the pool to her waist; a slim and not unattractive silhouette (if he overlooked her angular shoulders and the muck oozing down from the crown of her head and dribbling across her shoulders; those clotted lumps like supernumerary nipples sliding across her breasts...).

"Why did you make her?" she answered. Her voice was soft and glutinous, and lacked all emotion. "A glint in the eye; a clench in the balls...we all do as we please at the time."

"She was seven," he said, pain roiling in his guts. "She liked dressing up and dogs and making necklaces out of beads. She walked to school with her Mam and always ran ahead to the gate to see her friends. She hated having her hair brushed and wanted to be Rihanna."

Slowly she tilted her head, staring at him.

Rob drew himself more upright. "It was my job to put her to bed at night. She was a right good little reader, so she read her books to me. Then I'd put the light out and she'd always call me back, and I had to sing the daddy song to her." Dance to your daddy, my little lassie, dance to your daddy, when the boat comes in. She was scared about monsters under the bed, so he always set out Mr Paws and Chloe on her pillow, either side of her head, and told her that they would beat the stuffing out of any monster stupid enough to stick its nose into her room. That would make her smile, every time. "I told her I'd always look after her. I told her she was going to grow up tall and beautiful and clever, and she'd always be my girl." For a moment the words choked in his throat.

I lied, I lied. I wasn't there. She didn't get to grow up.

"Why would you do that? Why take her away from me?" he rasped.

She blinked, emerald eyes narrowed to slits. "I was hungry."

"You had no fucking right."

"I was hungry. I am always hungry. Dogs, rats, ducks...these things do not satisfy. It is centuries since you brought me gifts with honour and celebration. Why have you forgotten? Why have I had to wait?"

Yes—that was what he had half-remembered, from his own childhood. The warning—if you let your dog stray down into the Sleck, it would never come out. Back in those days dogs were just put out the front door in the morning to roam the streets and entertain themselves. Not like now. The roads were too busy now. Back in those days dogs just vanished, now and then. And there were stories, legends told avidly in back-garden dens and under the coat racks at school, of children who had gone missing too, at some vague unremembered point. But even after Bethany, when the journalists went looking, no one ever found documented proof of that.

"We took her away! You didn't eat her!"

"I ate the bit that mattered."

The hot sick rage in Rob's belly turned over and flared brighter. "You know what they're going to do here?" he asked savagely. "They've decided to fill this place in. For safety, like. They've finally decided to tell the environmentalists to go fuck themselves, and they're going to ship in tons of ash from the power station and bury this place. Tamp it down. Build it over. Houses. No Sleck anymore."

For a moment she seemed taken aback. Her eyes widened. Then she spoke, echoing him: "Houses." She grinned a little. Her teeth were mossy green and pointed, and the glisten of them made the dark pit of her mouth seem infinitely deep. "Children."

The ground seemed to sink under him, though he couldn't tell if that was physical reality or only his own senses. "Don't you fucking dare."

"Water rises, you know. Through ash and clay and pipes, through the cracks between bricks. Water finds its own level." She leaned in toward him, almost within reach. Rob thought how slender her neck looked. He could imagine how it would feel, cold and slick beneath his crushing hands. All his adult life he'd worked a steel-press, and his forearms were thick with muscle. He could imagine her narrow spine snapping like a swamp-rotted stick and her head falling away as he tore it from her shoulders. He imagined the plop it would make as it struck the water.

"You fucking bitch," he whispered. "You took my daughter. How do I go on without her?"

In she leaned, mouth twitching, her body angled from the water until Rob thought he ought to see waist and hips and not just more and more ribcage: a ribbon of slippery black goo. Her lips twitched hungrily.

"What's the point of my life now?" he complained softly. "What have I got to live for?"

"Then don't," she crooned, drooling a little. "Give up. Join her."

"Join her?"

"Down in the dark." Her pupil-less eyes were like green lamps now, lit with greed. "Among the sticks and the bones, soft and dark and safe and kept forever. Pearls shining in the night. Give me."

She was close enough.

"I'll give you," he grunted, and launched himself from his knees. Both hands shot forward and locked around her throat—and squeezed.

She made no sound. Beneath his fingers her oozing tar-flesh squashed and spurted; he had a moment of triumph before she thrashed backward from him, far stronger than he'd expected, and he staggered off the end of the pallet, feet sinking into the mud. But he didn't let go. Not even when she heaved round in the pool, dragging him this way and that. He could find no purchase with his feet at all, staggering and clinging, He saw her raised hands—those fingers far too long, looking like twigs dredged from the ooze at the bottom of a garden pond—and felt them lock about his own head, pushing it back and gouging at his face. Alcohol was the only thing that cushioned him from agony. He was determined to finish what he'd begun and choke her, but she didn't seem to feel any need to breathe. And she was stronger than him, he realised dimly through the beer-fug. She was bearing him over, forcing him onto his back. Her face was changing now, growing thinner and longer as the teeth pushed forward into an angler-fish snarl, while those pert little breasts were dissolving to slime and trickling down her torso.

She was too strong. Beneath his hands her throat was a twist of wet leather, boneless and vile. Her fingertips were jabbing his eyes. He wrenched his head from side to side, trying to escape her. His shoulders were in the water, and he screwed his eyes shut as great gobs of filth dripped from her hair onto his face.

Rob didn't see what it was that roared over his head. He just felt the air shake, and the woman's hands fly away, and then something smacked him down hard into the water, a glancing blow heavy enough to jar his own hands loose. For a moment the filthy water closed over his head and then he jerked out into the air again, gasping. He caught a glimpse of a heavy brown pelt, thick as the bristles on a broom-head, and a bulk that blocked out the sunlight—and he heard the swamp-maiden screech—but there was mud and blood on his face, filling his eye sockets, and nothing but mud beneath him, cold and viscous and sucking him down. He was sinking again, the slime trying to reclaim him. Rob thrashed over onto his belly, trying to swim, unable to get his face properly clear of the surface. Behind him a struggle was going on, but he could see nothing of it, not even who fought. There was mud in his mouth and up his nose, and it didn't take much down his throat to set him choking. He clawed for the pallet and couldn't find it. He grabbed at branches and green stems of the rushes but they broke beneath the force of his grasp.

He was drowning, he realised.

Then a hand closed around his wrist. For a moment he thought that it was her, back again—but the hand was small, though it had a grip like iron. It heaved him to the surface, pulling him until his face smacked up against the rough wood of the pallet. Rob grabbed at the slats, gasping for breath. Through lashes clotted with pond-slime he saw purple-striped tights on long slim legs, standing over him.

That was all.

By the time he pulled himself up onto the pallet, out of the sucking mud, and blinked and wiped his eyes clear, all was quiet. Slowly, still struggling to calm his heaving lungs, he looked around him. The surface of the little pond lay still once more, and the willows of the Sleck lifted indifferent arms to the sun. There was no black pond-lady. There was no furry animal bulk. There was no sign of whoever it was that had pulled him back to safety.

Just the doll Chloe, lying stained and limp on the slats. But Mr Paws the teddy had vanished altogether.

Rob picked up the rag doll and held it to his chest, his eyes wide. "Dance to your daddy," he whispered, "my little lassie."

# — POCOSIN —
## Ursula Vernon

*Author's note: Pocosins are a type of raised peat wetland found almost exclusively in the Carolinas. The name derives from an Eastern Algonquian word meaning "swamp on a hill." They are a rare and unique ecosystem, today widely threatened by development.*

This is the place of the carnivores, the pool ringed with sundews and the fat funnels of the pitcher plants.

This is the place where the ground never dries out and the loblolly pines grow stunted, where the soil is poor and the plants turn to other means of feeding themselves.

This is the place where the hairstreak butterflies flow sleekly through the air and you can hear insect feet drumming inside the bowl of the pitcher plants.

This is the place where the old god came to die.

He came in the shape of the least of all creatures, a possum. Sometimes he was a man with a long rat's tail, and sometimes he was a possum with too-human hands. On two legs and four, staggering, with his hands full of mud, he came limping through the marsh and crawled up to the witchwoman's porch.

"Go back," she said, not looking up. She had a rocking chair on the porch and the runners creaked as she rocked. There was a second chair, but she did not offer it to him. "Go back where you came from."

The old god laid his head on the lowest step. When he breathed, it hissed through his long possum teeth and sounded like he was dying.

"I'm done with that sort of thing," she said, still not looking up. She was tying flies, a pleasantly tricky bit of work, binding thread and chicken feathers to the wickedness of the hook. "You go find some other woman with witchblood in her."

The old god shuddered and then he was mostly a man. He crawled up two steps and sagged onto the porch.

The woman sighed and set her work aside. "Don't try to tell me you're dying," she said grimly. "I won't believe it. Not from a possum."

Her name was Maggie Grey. She was not so very old, perhaps, but she had the kind of spirit that is born old and grows cynical. She looked down on the scruffy rat-tailed god with irritation and a growing sense of duty.

His throat rasped as he swallowed. He reached out a hand with long yellow nails and pawed at the boards on the porch.

"Shit," Maggie said finally, and went inside to get some water.

She poured it down his throat and most of it went down. He came a little bit more alive and looked at her with huge, dark eyes. His face was dirty pale, his hair iron gray.

She knew perfectly well what he was. Witchblood isn't the same as godblood, but they know each other when they meet in the street. The question was why a god had decided to die on her porch, and that was a lousy sort of question.

"You ain't been shot," she said. "There's not a hunter alive that could shoot the likes of you. What's got you dragging your sorry ass up on my porch, old god?"

The old god heaved himself farther up on the porch. He smelled rank. His fur was matted with urine when he was a possum and his pants were stained and crusted when he was a man.

His left leg was swollen at the knee, a fat bent sausage, and the foot beneath it was black. There were puncture wounds in his skin. Maggie grunted.

"Cottonmouth, was it?"

The old god nodded.

Maggie sat back down in the rocking chair and looked out over the sundew pool.

There was a dense mat of shrubs all around the house, fetterbush and sheep laurel bound up together with greenbrier. She kept the path open with an axe, when she bothered to keep it open at all. There was no one to see her and the dying man who wasn't quite a man.

Mosquitos whined in the throats of the pitcher plants and circled the possum god's head. Maggie could feel her shoulders starting to tense up. It was always her shoulders. On a bad day, they'd get so knotted that pain would shoot down her forearms in bright white lines.

"Would've preferred a deer," she said. "Or a bear, maybe. Got some dignity that way." Then she laughed. "Should've figured I'd get a possum. It'd be a nasty, stinking sort of god that wanted anything to do with me."

She picked up a pair of scissors from where she'd been tying flies. "Hold still. No, I ain't gonna cut you. I ain't so far gone to try and suck the poison out of a god."

It had likely been another god that poisoned him, she thought—Old Lady Cottonmouth, with her gums as white as wedding veils. She saw them sometimes, big, heavy-bodied snakes, gliding easy through the water. Hadn't ever seen the Old Lady, but she was out there, and it would be just like a possum to freeze up when those white gums came at him, sprouting up fangs.

Even a witch might hesitate at that.

She waited until he was a man, more or less, and cut his pant leg open with the scissors. The flesh underneath was angry red, scored with purple. He gasped in relief as the tight cloth fell away from the swollen flesh.

"Don't thank me," she said grimly. "Probably took a few hours off your life with that. But they wouldn't be anything worth hanging on for."

She brought him more water. The first frogs began to screek and squeal in the water.

"You sure you want this?" she asked. "I can put a knife across your throat, make it easy."

He shook his head.

"You know who's coming for you?"

He nodded. Then he was a possum again and he gaped his mouth open and hissed in pain.

She hesitated, still holding the scissors. "Ain't sure I want to deal with 'em myself," she muttered. "I'm done with all that. I came out here to get *away*, you hear me?"

The possum closed his eyes, and whispered the only word he'd ever speak.

"...*sorry*..."

Maggie thrust the scissors into her pocket and scowled.

"All right," she said. "Let's get you under the porch. You come to me and I'll stand them off for you, right enough, but you better not be in plain sight."

She had to carry him down the steps. His bad leg would take no weight and he fell against her, smelling rank. There were long stains on her clothes before they were done.

Under the porch, it was cool. The whole house was raised up, to save it from the spring floods, when the sundew pool reached out hungry arms. There was space enough, in the shadow under the stairs, for a dying god smaller than a man.

She didn't need to tell him to stay quiet.

She went into the house and poured herself a drink. The alcohol was sharp and raw on her throat. She went down the steps again, to a low green stand of mountain mint, and yanked up a half dozen stems.

They didn't gentle the alcohol, but at least it gave her something else to taste. The frogs got louder and the shadows under the sheep laurel got thick. Maggie sat back in her rocking chair with her shoulders knotting up under her shirt and went back to tying flies.

Someone cleared his throat.

She glanced up, and there was a man in preacher's clothes, with the white collar and clean black pants. The crease in them was pressed sharp enough to draw blood.

"Huh," she said. "Figured the other one'd beat you here."

His gave her a pained, fatherly smile.

She nodded to the other chair. "Have a seat. I've got bad whiskey, but if you cut it with mint and sugar, it ain't bad."

"No, thank you," said the preacher. He sat down on the edge of the chair. His skin was peat colored and there was no mud on his shoes. "You know why I've come, Margaret."

"Maggie," she said. "My mother's the only one who calls me Margaret, and she's dead, as you very well know."

The preacher tilted his head in acknowledgment.

He was waiting for her to say something, but it's the nature of witches to outwait God if they can, and the nature of God to forgive poor sinners their pride. Eventually he said "There's a poor lost soul under your porch, Maggie Grey."

"He didn't seem so lost," she said. "He walked here under his own power."

"All souls are lost without me," said the preacher.

Maggie rolled her eyes.

A whip-poor-will called, placing the notes end to end, whip-er-*will!* whip-er-*will!*

It was probably Maggie's imagination that she could hear the panting of the god under the porch, in time to the nightjar's calls.

The preacher sat, in perfect patience, with his wrists on his knees. The mosquitos that formed skittering sheets over the pond did not approach him.

"What's there for a possum in heaven, anyway?" asked Maggie. "You gonna fill up the corners with compost bins and rotten fruit?"

The preacher laughed. He had a gorgeous, church-organ laugh and Maggie's heart clenched like a fist in her chest at the sound. She told her heart to behave. Witchblood ought to know better than to hold out hope of heaven.

"I could," said the preacher. "Would you give him to me if I did?"

Maggie shook her head.

His voice dropped, a father explaining the world to a child. "What good does it do him, to be trapped in this world? What good does it do anyone?"

"He seems to like it."

"He is a prisoner of this place. Give him to me and I will set him free to glory."

"He's a possum," said Maggie tartly. "He ain't got much use for glory."

The preacher exhaled. It was most notable because, until then, he hadn't been breathing. "You cannot doubt my word, my child."

"I ain't doubting nothing," said Maggie. "It'd be just exactly as you said, I bet. But he came to me because that's not what he wanted, and I ain't taking that away from him."

The preacher sighed. It was a more-in-sorrow-than-in-anger sigh, and Maggie narrowed her eyes. Her heart went back to acting the way a witch's heart ought to act, which was generally to ache at every damn thing and carry on anyway. Her shoulders felt like she'd been hauling stones.

"I could change your mind," he offered.

"Ain't your way."

He sighed again.

"Should've sent one of the saints," said Maggie, taking pity on the Lord, or whatever little piece of Him was sitting on her porch. "Somebody who was alive once, anyway, and remembers what it was like."

He bowed his head. "I will forgive you," he said.

"I know you will," said Maggie kindly. "Now get gone before the other one shows up."

Her voice sounded as if she shooed the Lord off her porch every day, and when she looked up again, he was gone.

It got dark. The stars came out, one by one, and were reflected in the sundew pool. Fireflies jittered, but only a few. Fireflies like grass and open woods, and the dense mat of the swamp did not please them. Maggie lit a lamp to tie flies by.

The Devil came up through a stand of yellowroot, stepping up out of the ground like a man climbing a staircase. Maggie was pleased to see that he had split hooves. She would have been terrible disappointed if he'd been wearing shoes.

He kicked aside the sticks of yellowroot, tearing shreds off them, showing ochre-colored pith underneath. Maggie raised an eyebrow at this small destruction, but yellowroot is hard to kill.

"Maggie Gray," said the fellow they called the Old Gentleman.

She nodded to him, and he took it as invitation, dancing up the steps on clacking hooves. Maggie smiled a little as he came up the steps, for the Devil always was a good dancer.

He sat down in the same chair that the preacher had used, and scowled abruptly. "See I got here late."

"Looks that way," said Maggie Gray.

He dug his shoulderblades into the back of the chair, first one then the other, rolling a little, like a cat marking territory in something foul. Maggie stifled a sigh. It had been a good rocking chair, but it probably wasn't wise to keep a chair around that the Devil had claimed.

"You've got something I want, Maggie Gray," he said.

"If it's my soul, you'll be waiting awhile," said Maggie, holding up a bit of feather. She looped three black threads around it, splitting the feather so it looked like wings. The hook gleamed between her fingers.

"Oh no," said the Devil, "I know better than to mess with a witch's soul, Maggie Gray. One of my devils showed up to tempt your great-grandmother, and she bit him in half and threw his horns down the well."

Maggie sniffed. "Well's gone dry," she said, trying not to look pleased. She knew better than to respond to demonic flattery. "It's the ground hereabouts. Sand and moss and swamps on top of hills. Had to dig another one, and lord knows how long it'll last."

"Didn't come here to discuss well-digging, Maggie Grey."

"I suppose not." She bit off a thread.

"There's an old god dying under your porch, Maggie Grey. The fellow upstairs wants him, and I aim to take him instead."

She sighed. A firefly wandered into a pitcher plant and stayed, pulsing green through the thin flesh. "What do you lot want with a scrawny old possum god, anyway?"

The Devil propped his chin on his hand. He was handsome, of course. It would have offended his notion of his own craftsmanship to be anything less. "Me? Not much. The fellow upstairs wants him because he's a stray bit from back before he and I were feuding. An old loose end, if you follow me."

Maggie snorted. "Loose end? The possum gods and the deer and Old Lady Cottonmouth were here before anybody thought to worship you. Either of you."

The Devil smiled. "Can't imagine there's many worshippers left for an old possum god, either. 'Cept the possums, and they don't go to church much."

Maggie bent her head over the wisp of thread and metal. "He doesn't feel like leaving."

Her guest sat up a little straighter. "I am not sure," he said, silky-voiced, "that he is strong enough to stop me."

Maggie picked up the pliers and bent the hook, just a little, working the feathers onto it. "He dies all the time," she said calmly. "You never picked him up the other times."

"Can only die so many times, Maggie Grey. Starts to take it out of you. Starts to make you tired, right down to the center of your bones. You know what that's like, don't you?"

She did not respond, because the worst thing you can do is let the Devil know when he's struck home.

"He's weak now and dying slow. Easy pickings."

"Seems like I might object," she said quietly.

The Devil stood up. He was very tall and he threw a shadow clear over the pool when he stood. The sundews folded their sticky leaves in where the shadow touched them. Under the porch steps, the dying god moaned.

He placed a hand on the back of her chair and leaned over her.

"We can make this easy, Maggie Gray," he said. "Or we can make it very hard."

She nodded slowly, gazing over the sundew pool.

"Come on—" the Devil began, and Maggie moved like Old Lady Cottonmouth and slammed the fish-hook over her shoulder and into the hand on the back of her chair.

The Devil let out a yelp like a kicked dog and staggered backwards.

"You come to *my* house," snapped Maggie, thrusting the pliers at him, "and you have the nerve to threaten me? A witch in her own home? I'll shoe your hooves in holy iron and throw *you* down the well, you hear me?"

"Holy iron won't be kind to witchblood," he gasped, doubled over.

"It'll be a lot less kind to *you*," she growled.

The Devil looked at his hand, with the fish-hook buried in the meat of his palm, and gave a short, breathless laugh. "Oh, Maggie Gray," he said, straightening up. "You aren't the woman your great-grandmother was, but you're not far off."

"Get gone," said Maggie. "Get gone and don't come back unless I call."

"You will eventually," he said.

"Maybe so. But not today."

He gave her a little salute, with the hook still stuck in his hand, and limped off the porch. The yellowroot rustled as he sank into the dirt again.

His blood left black spots on the earth. She picked up the lantern and went to peer at the possum god.

He was still alive, though almost all possum now. His whiskers lay limp and stained with yellow. There was white all around his eyes and a black crust of blood over his hind leg.

"Not much longer," she said. "Only one more to go, and then it's over. And we'll both be glad."

He nodded, closing his eyes.

On the way back onto the porch, she kicked at a black bloodstain, which had sprouted a little green rosette of leaves. A white flower coiled out of the leaves and turned its face to the moon.

"Bindweed," she muttered. "Lovely. One more damn chore tomorrow."

She stomped back onto the porch and poured another finger of whiskey.

It was almost midnight when the wind slowed, and the singing frogs fell silent, one by one.

Maggie looked over, and Death was sitting in the rocking chair.

"Grandmother," she said. "I figured you'd come."

"Always," said Death.

"If you'd come a little sooner, would've saved me some trouble."

Death laughed. She was a short, round woman with hair as gray as Maggie's own. "Seems to me you were equal to it."

Maggie grunted. "Whiskey?"

"Thank you."

They sat together on the porch, drinking. Death's rocker squeaked in time to the breathing of the dying god.

"I hate this," said Maggie, to no one in particular. "I'm tired, you hear me? I'm tired of all these fights. I'm tired of taking care of things, over and over, and having to do it again the next day." She glared over the top of her whiskey. "And don't tell me that it *does* make a difference, because I know that, too. Ain't I a witch?"

Death smiled. "Wouldn't dream of it," she said.

Maggie snorted.

After a minute, she said "I'm so damn tired of *stupid*."

Death laughed out loud, a clear sound that rang over the water. "Aren't we all?" she said. "Gods and devils, aren't we all?"

The frogs had stopped. So had the crickets. One whippoorwill sang uncertainly, off on the other side of the pond. It was quiet and peaceful and it would have been a lovely night, if the smell of the dying possum hadn't come creeping up from under the porch.

Death gazed into her mug, where the wilting mint was losing the fight against the whiskey. "Can't fix stupid," she said. "But other things, maybe. You feeling like dying?"

Maggie sighed. It wasn't a temptation, even with her shoulders sending bright sparks of pain toward her fingers and making the pliers hard to hold steady. "Feeling like resting," she said. "For a couple of months, at least. That's all I want. Just a little bit of time to sit here and tie flies and drink whiskey and let somebody else fight the hard fights."

Death nodded. "So take it," she said. "Nobody's gonna give it to you."

Maggie scowled. "I was," she said bitterly. "'Til a possum god showed up to die."

Death laughed. "It's why he came, you know," she said. Her eyes twinkled, just like Maggie's grandmother's had, when she wore the body that Death was wearing now. "He wanted to be left alone to die, so he found a witch that'd understand."

Maggie raked her fingers through her hair. "Son of a bitch," she said, to no one in particular.

Death finished her drink and set it aside. "Shall we do what's needful?"

Maggie slugged down the rest of the mug and gasped as the whiskey burned down her throat. "Needful," she said thickly. "That's being a witch for you."

"No," said Death, "that's being alive. Being a witch just means the things as need doing are bigger."

They went down the stairs. The boards creaked under Maggie's feet, but not under Death's, even though Death had heavy boots on.

Maggie crouched down and said "She's here for you, hon."

She would have sworn that the possum had no strength left in him, but he crawled out from under the porch, hand over hand. His hind legs dragged and his tail looked like a dead worm.

There was nothing noble about him. He stank and black fluid leaked from his ears and the corners of his eyes. Even now, Maggie could hardly believe that God and the Devil would both show up to bargain for such a creature's soul.

Death knelt down, heedless of the smell and the damp, and held out her arms.

The possum god crawled the last little way and fell into her embrace.

"There you are," said Death, laying her cheek on the spikey-furred forehead. "There you are. I've got you."

The god closed his eyes. His breath went out on a long, long sigh, and he did not draw another one.

Maggie walked away, to the edge of the sundew pool, and waited.

A frog started up, then another one. The water rippled as their throat sacs swelled. Something splashed out in the dark.

"It's done," called Death, and Maggie turned back.

The god look smaller now. Death had gathered him up and he almost fit in her lap, like a small child or a large dog.

"Don't suppose he's faking it?" asked Maggie hopefully. "They're famous for it, after all."

Death shook her head. "Even possum gods got to die sometime. Help me get him into the pond."

Maggie took him under the arms and Death took the feet. His tail dragged on the ground as they hauled him. Death went into the water first, sure-footed, and Maggie followed, feeling water come in over the tops of her shoes.

"If I'd been thinking, I would've worn waders," she said.

Death laughed Maggie's grandmother's laugh.

The bottom of the sundew pool was made of mud and sphagnum moss, and it wasn't always sure if it wanted to be solid or not. Every step she took required a pause while the mud settled and sometimes her heels sank in deep. She started to worry that she was going to lose her shoes in the pool, and god, wouldn't that be a bitch on top of everything else?

At least the god floated. Her shoulders weren't up to much more than that.

In the middle of the pool, Death stopped. She let go of the possum's feet and came around to Maggie's side. "This ought to do it," she said.

"If we leave the body in here, it'll stink up the pool something fierce," said Maggie. "There's things that come and drink here."

"Won't be a problem," Death promised. She paused. "Thought you were tired of taking care of things?"

"I am," snapped Maggie. "*Tired* isn't the same as *can't*. Though if this keeps up…"

She trailed off because she truly did not know what lay at the end of being tired and it was starting to scare her a little.

Death took the possum's head between her hands. Maggie put a hand in the center of his chest.

They pushed him under the water and held him for the space of a dozen heartbeats, then brought him to the surface.

"Again," said Death.

They dunked him again.

"Three times the charm," said Death, and they pushed him under the final time.

The body seemed to melt away under Maggie's hands. One moment it was a solid, hairy weight, then it wasn't. For a moment she thought it was sinking and her heart sank with it, because fishing a dead god out of the pond was going to be a bitch of a way to spend an hour.

But he did not sink. Instead he simply unmade himself, skin from flesh and flesh from bone, unraveling like one of her flies coming untied, and there was nothing left but a shadow on the surface of the water.

Maggie let out a breath and scrubbed her hands together. They felt oily.

She was freezing and her boots were full of water and something slimy wiggled past her shin. She sighed. It seemed, as it had for a long time, that witchcraft—or whatever this was—was all mud and death and need.

She was so damn tired.

She thought perhaps she'd cry, and then she thought that wouldn't much help, so she didn't.

Death reached out and took her granddaughter's hand.

"Look," said Death quietly.

Around the pond, the fat trumpets of the pitcher plants began to glow from inside, as if they had swallowed a thousand fireflies. The light cast green shadows across the surface of the water and turned the sundews into strings of cut glass beads. It cut itself along the leaves of the staggerbush and threaded between the fly-traps' teeth.

Whatever was left of the possum god glowed like foxfire.

Hand in hand, they came ashore by pitcher plant light.

Death stood at the foot of the steps. Maggie went up them, holding the railing, moving slow.

There were black stains on the steps where the god had oozed. She was going to have to scrub them down, pour bleach on them, maybe even strip the wood. The bindweed, that nasty little plant they called "Devil's Guts" was already several feet long and headed toward the mint patch. The stink of dying possum was coming up from under the steps and that was going to need to be scraped down with a shovel and then powdered with lime.

At least she could wait until tomorrow to take an axe to the Devil's rocking chair, though it might be sensible to drag it off the porch first.

The notion of all the work to be done made her head throb and her shoulders climb toward her ears.

"Go to bed, granddaughter," said Death kindly. "Take your rest. The world can go on without you for a little while."

"Work to be done," Maggie muttered. She held onto the railing to stop from swaying.

"Yes," said Death, "but not by you. Not tonight. I will make you this little bargain, granddaughter, in recognition of a kindness. I will give you a little time. Go to sleep. Things left undone will be no worse for it."

Death makes bargains rarely, and unlike the Devil, hers are not negotiable. Maggie nodded and went inside.

She fell straight down on the bed and was asleep without taking off her boots. She did not say goodbye to the being that wore her grandmother's face, but in the morning, a quilt had been pulled up over her shoulder.

The next evening, as the sun set, Maggie sat in her rocking chair and tied flies. Her shoulders were slowly, slowly easing. The pliers only shook a little in her hand.

She had dumped bleach over the steps, and the smell from under the porch had gone of its own accord. The bindweed...well, the black husks had definitely been bindweed, but something had trod upon it and turned it into ash. It was a kindness she hadn't expected.

Her whiskey bottle was also full, with something rather better than moonshine, although she suspected that a certain cloven-hooved gentleman might have been responsible for that.

The space on the porch where the other rocking chair had been ached like a sore tooth and caught her eye whenever she glanced over. She sighed. Still, the wood would keep the fire going for a couple of days, when winter came.

The throats of the pitcher plants still glowed, just a little. Easy enough to blame on tired eyes. Maggie wrapped thread around the puff of feather and the shining metal hook, and watched the glow from the corner of her eyes.

A young possum trundled out of the thicket, and Maggie looked up. "Don't start," she said warningly. "I'll get the broom."

The possum sat down on the edge of the pond. It was an awkward, ungainly little creature, with big dark eyes and wicked kinked whiskers. It was halfway hideous and halfway sweet, which gave it something in common with witches.

Slowly, slowly, the moon rose and the green light died away. The frogs chanted together in the dark.

The possum stood up, stretched, and nodded once to Maggie Gray. Then it shuffled into the undergrowth, its long rat-tail held behind it.

*I will give you a little time*, Death had said.

She wondered what Death considered 'a little time.' An hour? A day? A week?

"A few weeks," she said, to the pond and the absent possum. "A few weeks would be good. A little time for myself. The world can get on just fine without me for a couple of weeks."

She wasn't expecting an answer. The whippoorwills called to each other over the pond, and maybe that was answer enough.

Maggie poured two fingers of the Devil's whiskey, with hands that did not shake, and raised the glass in a toast to the absent world.

# BLUE AND GRAY
# — & BLACK AND GREEN —
## Alethea Kontis

*Keeping to the tradition of oral history in the hills, this story works best when read out loud, preferably to children around a campfire.*

Daniel was seven-and-three-quarters. He'd been seven-and-three-quarters forever. Daniel resided at Green Bottom, the one-armed General's big house on the river in Virginia. He liked tin whistles and marbles, especially the red ones. He liked his room at Green Bottom—he woke up every day in the same bed facing the window where the sunset shone through the trees. He liked the peppermint sticks the blue soldiers gave him when they rode through on their horses, though he missed the taste of candy. He liked the horses, too, the way the wind whipped through their manes and tails even when there was no wind. He liked the crazy Egyptian Lady, who wasn't really Egyptian but loved all things Egyptian and was still crazy and a Lady either way. He liked Mrs. Green, his sort-of nanny who kept the house. Daniel saw her as a thin woman with a white apron and bunned hair. The Shawnee saw her as an old woman with clay-red arms and eyes like stars. The slave children saw her as a fat woman with dusty hands and big white teeth. No matter what skin Mrs. Green wore, she always smelled of roses, which made him think of soap and summertime. Daniel liked summertime, and soap was so long ago he couldn't really remember it, but soap made things clean and he liked clean things, so he guessed he liked soap too.

In a way, Mrs. Green *was* the house, constantly herding the old spirits and ushering in the new. Daniel was one of these spirits, but Daniel had not died at Green Bottom. Mrs. Green told Daniel that he was a stone memory, a time of happiness and laughter that the bricks of Green Bottom held inside themselves so that they might draw more times of happiness into the house. Happiness does not want to stay in a place that is dark and lonely, so part of Daniel's job was to keep things from being dark and lonely. Mrs. Green was very wise.

Mrs. Green let Daniel play with the white children, the Shawnee children, and the slave children alike. Chieska, Young Fox, and Cold Water were best at stone tag. Polly, Suky, and the twins Isum and Eadom were best at jackstraws and scotch hoppers. Betsy was good at scotch hoppers too, and Thomas and William always played him at marbles. Daniel was best at playing hide-and-seek among the outbuildings. His best place to hide was the outhouse, since it had a window. He could peek through and see the other children coming through the wavy glass. He could see Mrs. Green through the window too, but he never hid for much longer after that. Mrs. Green did not suffer silly spirits. When it was time to come in it was time to come in, and Mrs. Green would not have him getting swept away in the river. Daniel did not like the river, with all its noisy rushing and pulling and grabbing. Daniel also did not like the black soldier.

He wasn't sure the black soldier was a soldier to begin with. Daniel had felt something watching him, and awoke to find a dark, swirling man-shaped mist by the window. Daniel said hello to the new spirit and invited him closer, but it just stayed that way, the tall shadow of a heavy object, though there were no objects standing by the window. Daniel tried to guess his name. He asked where the man was from and where he was going and if he had any family and if he missed them. Daniel talked to the shadow until he didn't feel like talking anymore. The shadow never moved or talked back. Until one day Daniel heard footsteps. He opened his eyes. The shadow had come closer.

Each time the shadow moved closer, Daniel could make out more details about his shape. The first thing Daniel noticed was the frock coat. There were two rows of buttons down the front, which meant the man was important, like General Jenkins. There was a sword belt and a buckle, but Daniel could not see the letters on the buckle. Too bad. Mrs. Green always gave him high marks on his letters. Daniel decided not to tell Mrs. Green about the soldier until he knew which side the soldier was on. If he was a blue soldier with the cavalry, Daniel would ask him for a peppermint stick. If he was a gray soldier, that meant he was mean, and Daniel would run and hide in his best hiding place and never look back.

The soldier grew a long black beard around his mouth that never spoke and his hollow eyes with no whites watched Daniel, always watching, but he never turned blue or gray. His clothes were black and stayed black, and his skin was blacker than Polly's and Suky's and Isum's and Eadom's put together, like a starless night, and the wind whistled through the cracks around the window but his hair never budged, and every time there were footsteps, he moved a little closer.

Daniel wondered if the man might be his father—Daniel's father had been a soldier. Isum and Eadom said that fathers were supposed to love their children and keep them safe. The way the black soldier watched Daniel did not make him feel loved or safe. It made him feel cold and hopeless. The way the man watched Daniel made him wonder if he had done something wrong. Maybe Mrs. Green had sent the soldier to deal with him if he stepped out of line. So Daniel did not step out of line. He stumbled through the scotch hoppers and leapfrog. He was ham-fisted with the marbles and the jackstraws. He was the first to be found in hide-and-seek and the first to line up when Mrs. Green came out to call for the children. Mrs. Green's roses smelled of love and safety. Daniel did not just like Green Bottom—he loved it. He did not want to leave.

Daniel wondered what the black soldier might do to punish him. Where did spirits go when they died? For that matter, where did memories go who were not really spirits to begin with? Thomas and Betsy assured him that God took care of all his children, even the ones who were never born and had never died. (William said that the black soldier would swallow Daniel whole and doom him to forevermore, but William was mean, so Daniel beat him soundly at marbles.) Polly and Suky and the slave twins told Daniel that the river would take him and turn his skin to tar and send him far away. Chieska and Young Fox and Cold Water told him that an old Shawnee woman would come for him and turn him into a doll and he would ride her dog into the clouds. The Egyptian Lady told Daniel that memory spirits were like smoke from an extinguished candle, rising up to the sky like a prayer hoping to find a god who would hold it to his or her breast. The Egyptian Lady also gave him gold foil coins and wore peanuts for earrings—but Daniel cracked the window so his smoke might escape and never again closed it, and the footsteps came ever closer.

Daniel eventually stopped playing with the children all together and stayed inside listening to the thunder. His mother had told him once that thunder was the angels bowling—at Green Bottom it was just General Jenkins bowling in the attic on the days when he had his good arm. It was a comforting sound. Daniel tried to stay up so late that late became early and early became late and he was confused as to whether up was down and back was forth and fell asleep anyway. Daniel tried to fall asleep in other rooms, but he always woke up in the same bed across from the same window. The black soldier was clearer now. Daniel could make out the eagle on his belt buckle and the stitches on his shoulder straps. He could see the red flames in those dark hollow eyes with no whites and he could feel their fire. Daniel could see the hole in the black soldier's coat where he had been shot in the chest so neatly that the buttons had not come undone. He could see the ragged skin there and the bloody broken bones beneath, all the way through to the black heart that did not beat. Daniel could smell the black soldier's breath and the tobacco made him remember how unpleasant vomiting had been.

The soldier did not do anything to Daniel. He only watched him and said nothing and made footsteps and came closer until when Daniel opened his eyes he could not see the room or the window at all, only black and fire and more black beneath that. If the black soldier came any closer he would be inside Daniel. Daniel did not want that blackness inside him.

Mrs. Green finally found Daniel inside the east chimney. It was his new best hiding place but there were no windows to keep a lookout so he did not see her coming. She pulled him out by the ear.

Daniel apologized over and over until the words sounded funny. He begged Mrs. Green not to send him away. Mrs. Green looked surprised. Mrs. Green never looked surprised. Daniel explained about the black soldier, and how he knew he was in trouble for something but he honestly didn't know what, and if she would only just please tell him, then he promised to stop doing it or start doing whatever it was immediately. Daniel knew it was his job to bring laughter to the house, but he didn't feel laughter inside himself anymore, and if he couldn't do his job then Green Bottom would not want him anymore and forget him.

Mrs. Green was not interested in Daniel's punishment; she was interested in the black soldier. She asked about his hat and the buttons on his coat. She asked about his sword belt and the buckle there. She asked about his long black beard and his fiery black eyes. She asked about the shotgun hole and his unbeating heart and his rotten teeth and his smell of tobacco. She asked about the footsteps, and how many there had been, and how long it had taken him to get from the window to Daniel's side. Daniel told her about all these things, all the things he thought about when he was inside and all the things he thought about while he was outside and all the things he thought about in between, and even some things he hadn't thought about yet at all but would now haunt him forever. And when Daniel had finished telling Mrs. Green all these things she kissed him on the forehead, told him to get some rest and not to worry, and shooed him off to bed like a good little boy.

Daniel went to bed, but he did not scoot there like a good little boy; he walked like a man to the hanging tree. He did not get any rest and he did worry. Daniel worried more right then than he had in his previous seven-and-three-quarters years and all the years after that combined. This would be his last night, his last day, his last moment. The black soldier would come and open his fleshy mouth with those rotting teeth and he would swallow Daniel whole, just one big gulp, and whatever was left of Daniel would be consumed in fiery blackness of forevermore. Daniel didn't like forevermore. Daniel liked Green Bottom in the springtime and running through the rooms and on the rooftop and spitting in the river and his old hiding place and his new hiding place and he was pretty sure forevermore had none of these things. It occurred to Daniel to be sad, and the feeling was so foreign it scared him all over again.

The black soldier opened his stinking rotten mouth, and opened and opened, and his jaw dropped and dropped and his head tilted back and back...and back...

And then Daniel saw Mrs. Green behind the soldier's head, her strong knuckly fingers around the hair at the back of his neck. She made mention of his rudeness, and how visitors in a fine house should always introduce themselves properly. And then she tore his face off. Flames engulfed Daniel's hands, but they did not hurt him so he did not scream, but that was okay because the soldier screamed enough for them both. His skin split as if it were made of spun sugar, the halves of it shredding apart at the rend like cobwebs. Despite the blood in his wound there was no blood in the heart of him, nor was there the neverending fiery darkness of forevermore as William the Meanie had suggested. But there were teeth and wiry hair and tentacles. Lots and lots of slimy tentacles, reaching and throbbing and flailing. And suddenly Daniel did know him.

Daniel had not recognized the face of the soldier, but he recognized the monster inside him. That monster had lived in his closet when he was much younger than his seven-and-three-quarters years. It had lived under his bed, and it had lived in his dreams, and if the Daniel he was now existed because the bricks of Green Bottom had kept a happy memory, how had he brought the irrational fears with him?

But there was no time for that now. They could talk about that later when there wasn't a giant writhing monster full of teeth screaming and roaring and sliming the floorboards and mussing Mrs. Green's perfect hair.

Mrs. Green's other hand reached inside the mass of tentacles and somehow silenced the creature. Daniel could now hear what Mrs. Green was saying. She calmly explained that benevolent spirits were welcome and chaotic spirits were not, and that the monster was free to haunt anywhere as long as that place was not Green Bottom. She reminded the monster never to follow Daniel's spirit thread back through the ether, and that the ghosts of Green Bottom were going to destroy him now. No hard feelings, of course, it was just the way they did things here. Green Bottom looked after its own.

The General was the first to appear, both arms intact, and after shooting the monster without hesitation he pulled free his sword and removed whatever tentacles managed to come within reach. The Shawnee came with their arrows. The slaves came with their scythes. The Egyptian Lady clawed at its eyes, when there were eyes. The children amassed behind Daniel and threw marbles at the beast. William pushed a handful of marbles into Daniel's fist and, with a war cry, Daniel joined them. Piece by piece the monster came apart, and when the black shadows pieced it back together, the ghosts of Green Bottom took it apart again. Daniel wasn't sure the fight would ever end…and then he heard the horn of the cavalry.

The horses made quick work of the beast; slime became foam on their nostrils and flesh melted into fog beneath their hooves. Swords sliced tentacles sideways and teeth fell to the floorboards like rain. Soft rain. Happy rain.

The next day, Daniel enjoyed waking up across from the window in his shadowless room. He lost to Betsy and Suky at scotch hoppers, and beat William soundly again at marbles (though William might have let him win), and when it was time for hide-and-seek he crawled up into his new hiding place in the east chimney. It might not have had a window but he was surrounded by bricks, the bricks of Green Bottom that remembered his happiness so fondly, and he felt safe as houses.

# ACKNOWLEDGEMENTS

Special thanks to Jessica Corra-Larter, Travis Heerman, Camille Griep, Margaret McGraw, Adrienne Dellwo, and all the wonderful people who have supported, backed, helped, or simply put up with me.

# ABOUT THE AUTHORS

**Steven S. Long** is a writer and game designer who's worked primarily in the tabletop roleplaying game field for the past twenty years. During that time he's written or co-written nearly 200 books. He's best known for his work with Champions and the HERO System, but has worked for many other RPG companies. In recent years he's branched out into writing fiction as well, contributing Fantasy short stories to numerous anthologies. He frequently claims that he's revising his novel, but this may be an elaborate scam of some sort. His first major work of non-fiction, a book on the Norse god Odin for Osprey Publishing, was released in May 2015. His Master Plan for World Domination has reached Stage 67-Zeta. You can find out more about Steve and what he's up to at *www.stevenslong.com*.

**Sarah Goslee** wants to know everything, and then to tell everyone else about it. She's a scientist because that's how you learn things that nobody else knows, writes fiction and nonfiction indiscriminately, makes things out of string, and dresses like a Viking on weekends. She writes about science, fiction, and other obsessions at *www. sarahgoslee.com*.

**Sunil Patel** is a Bay Area fiction writer and playwright who has written about everything from ghostly cows to talking beer. His plays have been performed at San Francisco Theater Pub and San Francisco Olympians Festival, and his fiction has appeared in *Saturday Night Reader, Fireside Magazine,* and *The Book Smugglers.* Plus, he reviews books for *Lightspeed,* and he is Assistant Editor of *Mothership.* Find out more at ghostwritingcow.com, where you can watch his plays, or follow him @ghostwritingcow. His Twitter has been described as "engaging," "exclamatory," and "crispy, crunchy, peanut buttery."

**Chaz Brenchley** has been making a living as a writer since the age of eighteen. He is the author of nine thrillers, including *Shelter*; two fantasy series, "The Books of Outremer" and "Selling Water by the River"; and two ghost stories, *House of Doors* and *House of Bells.* As Daniel Fox, he has published a Chinese-based fantasy series, beginning with *Dragon in Chains*, and as Ben Macallan an urban fantasy series, beginning with *Desdaemona.* A British Fantasy Award winner, he has also published books for children and more than 500 short stories in various genres. His time as crimewriter-in-residence on a sculpture project in Sunderland resulted in the earlier collection *Blood Waters*. His first play, *A Cold Coming*, premiered and toured in 2007. He is a prizewinning ex-poet, and has been writer in residence at the University of Northumbria. He was Northern Writer of the Year 2000. Chaz has recently married and moved from Newcastle to California, with two squabbling cats and a famous teddy bear.

**James Lowder** has worked extensively on both sides of the editorial blotter. As a writer his publications include the bestselling, widely translated dark fantasy novels *Prince of Lies* and *Knight of the Black Rose*, short fiction for such anthologies as *Shadows Over Baker Street* and *Truth Until Paradox*, and comic book scripts for DC, Image, Moonstone, and Desperado. As an editor he's directed novel lines or series for both large and small publishing houses, and has helmed more than a dozen critically acclaimed anthologies, including *Madness on the Orient Express, Hobby Games: The 100 Best*, and the "Books of Flesh" zombie trilogy. His work has received five Origins Awards and an ENnie Award, and been a finalist for the International Horror Guild Award and the Stoker Award.

**Andy Duncan** has won a Nebula Award, a Theodore Sturgeon Memorial Award and three World Fantasy Awards, including for the novella "Wakulla Springs," written with Ellen Klages (Tor.com, 2013). His third collection, *An Angel of Utopia: New and Selected Stories* was published by Small Beer in 2016. His stories have appeared in magazines including *Asimov's, Clarkesworld, Conjunctions, The Magazine of Fantasy & Science Fiction*, and *Weird Tales*; in anthologies including the "Eclipse," "Starlight" and "Living Dead" series; and in multiple year's-best volumes. A Clarion West graduate, he has taught Clarion West twice (2005 and 2015) and Clarion twice (2004 and 2013) and is a member of the permanent Sturgeon Award jury. He is a tenured associate professor in the English department at Frostburg State University, where he coordinates the journalism minor and is faculty adviser to the independent student news organization, The Bottom Line. A native of Batesburg, South Carolina, he lives in Frostburg, Maryland, with his wife, Sydney.

**Vivienne Pustell** is a graduate student at Stanford University and a former high school English teacher. She has presented her fiction at San Francisco's Litquake and to her cat. This is her first publication.

**Scott Edelman** has published more than 85 short stories in magazines such as *Postscripts, The Twilight Zone, Absolute Magnitude, The Journal of Pulse-Pounding Narratives, Science Fiction Review* and *Fantasy Book*, and in anthologies such as *Why New Yorkers Smoke, The Solaris Book of New Science Fiction: Volume Three, Crossroads: Southern Tales of the Fantastic, Men Writing SF as Women, MetaHorror, Once Upon a Galaxy, Moon Shots, Mars Probes, Forbidden Planets, Summer Chills, The Mammoth Book of Monsters,* and *The Monkey's Other Paw: Revived Classic Stories of Dread and the Dead.*

A collection of his horror fiction, *These Words Are Haunted* came out from Wildside Books in 2001, and a standalone novella *The Hunger of Empty Vessels* was published in 2009 by Bad Moon Books. He is also the author of the Lambda Award-nominated novel *The Gift* (Space & Time, 1990) and the collection *Suicide Art* (Necronomicon, 1992). His collection of zombie fiction, *What Will Come After,* came in 2010 from PS Publishing, and was a finalist for both the Stoker Award and the Shirley Jackson Memorial Award. His science fiction short fiction has been collected in *What We Still Talk About* from Fantastic Books.

He has been a Stoker Award finalist five times, both in the category of Short Story and Long Fiction. Additionally, Edelman worked for the Syfy Channel for more than thirteen years as editor of *Science Fiction Weekly, SCI FI Wire,* and *Blastr.* He was the founding editor of *Science Fiction Age,* which he edited during its entire eight-year run. He also edited *SCI FI* magazine, previously known as *Sci-Fi Entertainment,* for more a decade, as well as two other SF media magazines, *Sci-Fi Universe* and *Sci-Fi Flix.* He has been a four-time Hugo Award finalist for Best Editor.

**Thoraiya Dyer** is an award-winning Australian writer. Her short science fiction and fantasy has appeared in *Clarkesworld, Apex, Analog, Nature,* and *Cosmos,* among others (for a full list, see www.thoraiyadyer.com ). Her collection of four original stories, *Asymmetry,* available from Twelfth Planet Press, was called "unsettling, poignant, marvellous" by Nancy Kress. A lapsed veterinarian, her other interests include bushwalking, archery and travel. The first book in her "Titan's Forest" trilogy debuted from Tor books in 2017.

**Steven H Silver** has worked as a writer, reviewer, editor, and publisher. His stories have appeared in Black Gate, Helix, and various anthologies. He was the founder and original editor and publisher of ISFiC Press and has also edited books for DAW Books and NESFA Press. Steven also serves as SFWA's Events Manager.

**Keris McDonald** lives in the not-very-grim north of England and has seen her horror short stories published in *All Hallows* magazine and anthologies by Ashtree Press and Hic Dragones Books. Her story "The Coat Off His Back" appears in *Best Horror of the Year, vol.7* (ed. Ellen Datlow). However, she spends most of her writing time under the pen name, Janine Ashbless, spinning tales of supernatural erotica and passionate romantic adventure for publishers such as HarperCollins and Virgin. Her ninth novel, *Cover Him with Darkness*, a tale of fallen angels and religious conspiracy, was published in 2014 by Cleis Press. "The Sleck" was inspired by the post-industrial landscape of County Durham and childhood memories of visiting her aunts and uncles in Newcastle, as well as stories of "sacred" wells and springs. "Sleck," by the way, is a very old dialect word for "stinking mud."

**Anatoly Belilovsky** is a Russian-American author and translator of speculative fiction. His work appeared in the *Unidentified Funny Objects* anthology, *Ideomancer, Nature Futures, Stupefying Stories, Immersion Book of Steampunk, Mammoth Book of Dieselpunk, Daily SF, Kasma, Kazka,* and has been podcast by *Cast of Wonders, Tales of Old,* and *Toasted Cake.* He was born in a city that went through six or seven owners in the last century, all of whom used it to do a lot more than drive to church on Sundays; he is old enough to remember tanks rolling through it on their way to Czechoslovakia in 1968. After being traded to the US for a shipload of grain and a defector to be named later (see Wikipedia, Jackson-Vanik amendment), he learned English from Star Trek reruns and went on to become a pediatrician in an area of New York where English is only the fourth most commonly used language. He has neither cats nor dogs, but was admitted into SFWA in spite of this deficiency. He blogs about writing at loldoc.net.

A noted video game and tabletop RPG writer, **Richard Dansky** is also the author of six novels and the short fiction collection *Snowbird Gothic.* He has written for numerous games including *Tom Clancy's Splinter Cell: Blacklist, Ghost Recon: Future Soldier* and the original *Far Cry,* and was named one of the Top 20 Game Writers by *Gamasutra* in

2009. He is currently working on the 20th anniversary edition of the critically acclaimed tabletop *RPG Wraith: The Oblivion*. A long-time resident of Durham, NC, he lives with his wife and their variably-sized collections of books, My Little Ponies, and single malt scotches.

Bestselling and award-winning author **Alethea Kontis** is a princess, fairy godmother, and geek. She has dabbled in novels, picture books, poetry, essays, online video rants, and making horror movies. Princess Alethea lives on the Space Coast of Florida with her teddy bear, Charlie.

**Ursula Vernon** is the author and illustrator of far more projects than is probably healthy. She has written over fifteen books for children, several novels for adults, an epic webcomic called "Digger" and various short stories and other odds and ends. "Digger" won the Hugo Award for Best Graphic Story (2012) and the Mythopoeic Fantasy Award (2013). Her short stories and children's fiction have been nominated for and won awards including the Nebula for Best Short Story, the Coyotl Award, the WSFA Small Press Award, the Sequoyah Award for Children's Literature, the Amelia Bloomer List for feminist children's literature. Her stand-alone novel *Castle Hangnail* won the Mythopoeic Fantasy Award for Children's Literature in 2016, and her novelette "The Tomato Thief" won the Hugo Award for Best Novelette in 2017. Her current project is the *Hamster Princess* series of books for kids. She also writes for adults under the name T. Kingfisher. You can find her online at *redwombatstudio.com*.